MW00736946

NO TURNING BACK

NO TURNING BACK

STORIES

[signature: Dan Burns]

DAN BURNS

CHICAGO ARTS PRESS

Chicago

ISBN: 978-0-9911694-0-5
Library of Congress Control Number: 2014903777

Cover art, illustration, and design by *Hugh Syme*
Interior illustrations by *Kelly Maryanski*
Book design by *Vasil Nazar*
Author photo by *Kate Burns*

Published and printed in the United States of America by
CHICAGO ARTS PRESS
www.chicagoartspress.com

Author information:
www.danburnsauthor.com
dan@danburnsauthor.com

9 8 7 6 5 4 3 2

First Edition

As always, this one is for
Lorraine, Katie, and David

CONTENTS

INTRODUCTION

It all started with a thought.

Over the years, I have often found that in order to get an idea to come to fruition, all I needed to do was think about the idea—that's it, just think. The more I would think about an idea, the more my conscious and subconscious brain would join in to help develop and flesh it out. Thoughts would turn into other ideas, which would make me think even more, and before I knew it, I had a plan in place to make the idea a reality. That is how it has been with my writing in general, and with my short stories in particular: I get an idea, store it in my head to let it simmer a while, and write the story when it is ready.

Twenty-five years ago, I first considered becoming a writer and have been thinking about that idea ever since. My favorite authors— Bradbury, Crichton, Fitzgerald, Hemingway, Harrison, and King— had made me do it. Think, that is. Over the years, they had grabbed me and engaged me with their words and especially their short stories. They opened my eyes to the limitless possibilities of words and books. Particularly through the influence of their short stories, they urged me to keep reading, and by all means, to start writing.

I have always enjoyed the short story form. Unlike reading a novel, reading a short story impacts me more immediately. I love getting through an entire story in one sitting and then moving on to the next one. When reading a short story collection, I can get a fuller picture of the thoughts and ideas that the author has in store for me.

One book in particular—and a subsequent meeting with the author—set me on my way to becoming a writer. The book was *Dandelion Wine*, written by one of the greatest American authors, Ray Bradbury. I had read other Bradbury books, like *Fahrenheit 451* and *The Martian Chronicles*, but when I read *Dandelion Wine*, which is actually a series of loosely connected short stories, it was the first time I could truly visualize the overarching story as I read it. It was the first time I became part of the story. It was the first time I experienced words and sentences strung together in such a unique way: literature with doses of realism and lyrics and poetics. He hooked me. I thought to myself, *I want to be able to write a book like that some day*. I'm a big dreamer.

In 2003, while in San Diego on business, I had the opportunity to meet Ray Bradbury. I had heard about a seminar he was conducting at San Diego State University and on a whim, I changed my afternoon plans to attend. His two-hour talk about his "love of writing" was truly inspirational, and his words made me wonder even more about becoming a career writer. Afterward, I met Ray, and he signed a book for me. He asked me if I was a writer, and I told him that I wanted to be one someday. He said, "Just do it," and I replied, "Okay, I will." Four years later, I became a writer. Although I had been writing for years, I made it official, with a total commitment to writing and to publishing my writing.

My fiction writing took off at a feverish pace. I focused mostly on shorter pieces, which allowed me to flesh out many ideas with a minimal investment of time and get the writing practice I needed. I get many ideas for writing projects, and I usually try to see if the idea is worthwhile by attacking it through a short piece, such as a poem or a short story. After that, if I still like the idea and the premise, I will consider it for a longer form.

For example, I wrote *Letting Go*—a story in this collection—as a way to explore the character of Sebastian Drake, to better understand exactly who he was and what made him tick. After I wrote the short story, I was more interested in Drake—and perplexed by him—than ever, and I needed to find out where he was going next. That was not a problem. He would not leave me alone, so I put him in Chicago, right in the middle of a cold murder case, and a year later I completed the screenplay *A Fine Line,* with Drake in the lead role. I thought that might be the end of his story, but that was not the case. Drake persisted, even insisted, that the story was not over, and he was right. I completed the full story of *A Fine Line,* in novel form, a year after the screenplay. I wonder where he will take me next.

People often ask me how I came up with a certain idea or why I decided to write a particular story. Those are tough questions to answer. All I can say is that ideas come, at any time of the day or night, and it is usually something I saw or read or heard that inspired them. The ideas come, and when they do, it is prudent for me to jot them down so I do not forget them. I realize there is a reason the ideas come to me, and it is not up to me to judge the source. However, it is up to me to trust the source, because the ideas germinate from the combined experiences of my lifetime. The ideas are *me*. I think it is true that I do not have a say in which stories I write. I do not write a story because I think it will lead to fame or fortune. I write a story because I have to, because the idea nags at me and will not leave me alone until the words are down onto the page and the story is finished.

I took the title for this book from the final story in this collection. *No Turning Back* is actually the first story I wrote, and the story is about a man put in a predicament where the only option is to jump forward, into the unknown and on to whatever comes next. I had no prior intention, but as I was pulling together the stories for this book, it was clear to me that all of the stories were linked by a similar theme: that every day we come to a crossroads in life and going back the way we came is not an option. *No Turning Back* is not only a fitting title for the book, but it also provides a sound mantra for living our lives: don't try to re-live the past, for the future has so much in store for us. Just keep moving forward.

In preparing this collection, I thought quite a bit about the stories and the sequence in which I might like to present them. I wrote the stories in this collection over a period of six years, from August 2006 to September 2012. In the end, it made sense for me to present the stories chronologically. However, I knew I did not want to start with the first story. That story, *No Turning Back*, holds a special place in my heart and I felt it best to end with that story. Therefore, we begin with the most recent story and progress in reverse chronological order to the first story written. We'll jump into our figurative time machine and as we progress through the stories, we'll take a journey to see where I came from. We'll make many stops along the way to discover what might have been going on in my mind and my life at the time. I hope you enjoy the ride.

With this book, I wanted to produce something different, more than just words on a page. Of course, the stories are important, but I wanted to provide a broader experience for the reader. I have always been particularly fond of books that combined words with art as many of the early Dickens novels in my book collection did, with exquisite woodcut illustrations that graced the pages preceding a chapter. Unfortunately, that type of illustration is a lost art and is no longer financially feasible. Recently, I had been particularly impressed with the work of Joseph Mugnaini, the artist who provided many illustrations for Ray Bradbury's novels and story collections. I thought it would be great to include illustrations in my book.

I set out to find an illustrator, and I was fortunate to meet Chicago actor and artist Kelly Maryanski, who read the manuscript and provided custom ink illustrations for each of the stories. I had talked with a half dozen artists, and I think she was the only one who really understood what I was trying to accomplish. I sent her the manuscript and waited, wondering what was going to happen next. Her approach was simple and straightforward. She read a story and then sent over an illustration for me to review. I received each illustration with anticipation and excitement, and every time I saw the newest one, I smiled. Every reader interprets a story differently, but Kelly and I were always on the same page. I think each of the illustrations is perfect, and each story now includes an original and thought-provoking visual interpretation.

I also felt I needed a book cover that would help to capture the essence of the book and set it apart visually. From the day I came home from the record store with Rush's *2112* album as a teenager, I was hooked on my favorite band's album art and the graphic artistry of Hugh Syme. When I thought about the cover art for this book, I felt the artwork had to be something special, much like *2112* and all of the Rush albums since, and I thought about how great it would be to have Hugh Syme design my book cover. *No chance in hell,* I thought. It was a pipe dream, but I figured, *what the hell.* I contacted him. I told him I was a fan of his work, and it would be an honor if he would design my book cover. He asked me about the book, and I shared with him the title, the story names, and a brief description of each story. He said "okay" and that was that. A week later, he sent me three designs. The first one was great, the second one better, and when I got to the third image, I knew I had found my book cover. He insisted that he be part of the entire jacket design and the final production, and it was a privilege to work with such a consummate professional. What an experience and what a trip it was.

There was one final element that I wanted to include in the book. I don't know about you, but after I've read a story, I'm often left with burning questions: what was the inspiration for the story, where did the original idea come from, and what was going on in the author's head while writing the story? The only way I have been able to get answers to these questions is if I've had the opportunity to meet the author in person. Such a meeting almost never happens, and even if it does, it's hard to ask the questions. More often than not, the answers remain elusive.

I decided I was not going to be so elusive. There is so much that goes into the writing of a story, and because every story in this collection is so different, I thought it might be nice to share with the reader whatever was going on inside my head at the time. From the day I first started writing short stories, I got into the practice of documenting my story ideas, along with other thoughts, conceptions, and notes that pertained to the story. I did it for myself, to help me remember. However, as I went through my old notes, I was surprised to learn about my younger self and the mania that was coursing through my veins. *Where did those ideas and words come from?* I often wondered. The process of reviewing my story notes was a great opportunity to re-introduce myself to the individual who wrote the stories, stories that were—quite simply—distant memories. The notes brought the stories back to me in all their glory, and I hope the story notes provide for the reader a small glimpse into the mind of a hopeful author.

No Turning Back is a book quite different from my first novel, *Recalled to Life*, and even more drastically different from my first non-fiction book, *The First 60 Seconds*. I like that. Diversity is good for me. In the future, I have every intention of following my brain and my gut as I select new writing projects. So, you may be wondering, *what's next?* My first crime novel, *A Fine Line,* is set for publication next year. Am I writing poetry? Yes. Are there more screenplays to come (hopefully to the big screen)? Absolutely. Will there be more short stories and novels? Yes and yes. What I do know is that I have enough ideas to keep me writing for at least another ten years. I cannot say I am certain of the order and form in which I will produce my ideas, but I can say, with absolute certainty, that I will write. I cannot fight it, I have no other choice, and there is absolutely no turning back.

Dan Burns
January 2014

NO TURNING BACK

STORIES

Each breath we take brings us to, and past,

a crossroads in life, and there is

no turning back.

Come Out, Wherever You Are

Some unknown and unseen force had granted his ultimate wish. He was alone, sitting a bit uncomfortably with his solitude and silence, his thoughts and his books, wondering whether he had any right to make such a wish in the first place. Just two months earlier, the world had been a very different place. Vernon Parrish had been different. His friends, neighbors, and all of the townspeople had been of a quite different form and perspective as well. While his past was sometimes unbearable, life for Vernon Parrish had been normal, as far as he could recall, when compared with the most recent of his seventy-two years on this earth. Now he struggled to make sense of it all.

Verne, as people knew him, had traveled to the town of Livingston, Montana for an initial visit on a parched and dusty summer after-noon not quite six years ago. As he drove into town that first day, it was love at first sight, and he never left. He had just retired as the mayor of a large suburb just outside of Chicago, and he went to Montana for peace and solitude, and to get out of the public eye. He went for the mountains, the big sky and, of course, he went for the rivers.

Verne's celebrity went with him, which he accepted since he realized he would never be able to fully escape the notoriety and attention from his past life. As mayor, he walked the streets of his town at any hour of the day or night, and people recognized him instantly. Cameras flashed often and his every action and word was captured for some later public distribution, consumption, and criticism. However, in Montana it was different. Though he became well known immediately and was respected for his broad smile and generous, outgoing personality, the townspeople of Livingston respected his privacy and cared only about the present. Many people in town, especially those who did not know him well, called him "Mayor," both out of respect and because it was an easy name to remember. Verne didn't mind. He quickly realized that the people of Montana were sincerely the nicest people of any place he had visited in his lifetime.

It was two months ago that Verne went into town, the town as he had come to know it, for the last time. Every other morning for almost six years, after walking along the river with his golden retriever, Buddy, he would put the dog in the cab of his truck and drive into town for breakfast, a visit, and to pick up any supplies he might need. On that one particular and final day, a cold and windy day in May, he pulled up in front of the diner and immediately suspected that something was amiss. Everything *looked* right to him—the façade of the diner, the cars parked in the street, and the few scattered pedestrians walking along the sidewalk—but something didn't *feel* right. He cracked a window, gave Buddy a Milk-Bone, and got out of his truck. He stood for a moment, looked, and listened as he chewed on a fingernail, but no revelation was forthcoming. He walked into the diner.

"Mornin', Verne," said Bob Harrison, the proprietor, who stood behind the counter and wiped the worn linoleum anxiously. He did not look at Verne.

"Bob," Verne said. He walked along the full length of the counter and took his usual stool at the end near the paneled wall. He sat down on the diner stool, which was secured into the floor, and he spun around to observe the other patrons. It was then that he realized everyone had stopped talking, and he saw the many stolid and concerned faces pointed in his direction.

Bob walked up to Verne casually, set a cup down, and poured it full to the brim with steaming coffee. He turned to walk away.

Verne caught him. "Bob?"

Bob turned. "Yeah, Verne?"

"A menu, please?"

Bob walked down to the end of the counter, grabbed a menu from the top of the stack, and walked back over. He set the menu down in front of Verne.

"What gives?" Verne said. "Feels like a morgue in here. Someone die?"

Bob shook his head, and his face showed disappointment.

"What is it, for Pete's sake?" Verne was growing more uncomfortable with each passing second.

"You see the paper this morning?" Bob asked.

"Not yet."

Bob reached below the counter and pulled out a newspaper. He held it with both hands, head down, and stared silently at the front page.

"You gonna let me see it?" Verne asked.

Bob continued his downward stare and shook his head once again.

"Bob, how long have we been friends now? How many mornings have I come in here to have breakfast and read your newspaper? Hand it over."

Bob set the paper down on the counter, turned it around, and slid it over to Verne.

"Son of a bitch," Verne said. There in front of him, in a four-by-six photograph, was Vernon Parrish as a much younger man. Beneath the picture, in bold black letters, was the headline, "Ex-Mayor with a Sordid Past."

"Son of a bitch," Verne repeated, as a dormant anger rose up within him. His chest bulged, and heat and blood rose to his head and flushed his face. He looked at Bob, who was staring at him.

"Never thought *you'd* have any enemies," Bob said.

"I guess I do now."

"Don't want to believe it, Verne, but . . ."

"But what?" Verne said.

"It *is* right there in the paper, plain as puddin'."

Verne shoved the paper off the counter, spun off the stool, and stormed out of the diner. He saw many judgmental eyes tracking his departure, and he judged them silently in return. Once outside, he took a deep breath and looked through the windshield of his truck. Buddy was sitting up on the front seat, his tongue wagging in anticipation. The dog would have to wait. Verne crossed the street with a determined stride, headed down a half block, and turned the corner. Another half block down was the office of *The Livingston Herald.* He entered the building and stepped inside the first office he came upon. He found Karen Shultz and Ted McNamara, both standing behind a large wooden worktable, shuffling photographs and random sheets of a newspaper. Ted was the newspaper editor, and Karen was his copyeditor.

"What the hell is going on?" Verne said.

"Whatever do you mean?" Ted replied, a tad pompous.

"Don't screw with me, Ted. You know exactly what I'm talking about. The morning paper—the front page."

"Oh, that."

Verne stepped forward aggressively, the rage building inside of him.

"Take it easy, Verne." Ted turned to Karen. "Would you excuse us for a moment?" Karen left the room, and Ted continued. "Verne, we're in the news business." He picked up a copy of the morning edition and turned it to show Verne. "And this is news."

"It's bullshit, and you know it." Verne clenched his jaw tight and balled up his fists. He relaxed his jaw only enough to get out, "It was over *thirty* years ago."

"That's true, but we have no statute of limitations here in the newspaper business. We now have access to most everything about everyone and about any little thing that might have happened during the course of a person's lifetime. Our lives are an open book for everyone to read, and everything about everyone has the potential to be news, if not now, then maybe sometime in the future."

"But it's not true!" Verne shouted.

"Says you. Verne, if you have information to the contrary, I'll be happy to look at it. If I'm wrong, I'll print a retraction."

"Guilty until proven innocent?" Verne said.

"It's just the nature of the news business these days. The people want the news, the information, and it's our job to give it to them."

"You son of a bitch." Verne squeezed his fists tightly and his knuckles cracked. He grunted and stepped up closer to the table. He could see the concern in Ted's eyes.

"Karen," Ted shouted. "Call the sheriff, please." To Verne he said, "Don't make this any worse for yourself."

Verne watched Ted's lips move but heard nothing. With two hands, he grabbed the underside of the table and in one swift and violent motion, he flipped the table over onto its side and toward Ted. If Ted had not reacted and stepped backward when he did, the edge of the table would likely have come down on his toes, pulverizing the bones into dust.

"You crazy old coot!" Ted shouted.

Verne flashed a sinister grin and stared at Ted with steely eyes. A flash of fear replaced the concern reflected in Ted's eyes. Verne wondered if Ted might have pissed himself. The thought made him feel better, and he turned and left.

Only thirty minutes had passed since the incident at the diner, but Verne already had a plan cemented in place and in full motion. Verne likely always had the plan but simply needed the circumstance to call it into action. He had driven across town and out south on Route 89 to his first and only planned destination before heading home. He pulled into the empty gravel parking lot of Pete's General Store and stirred up quite a dust cloud. His truck came to rest at the front entrance, lightly bumping the old horse tie-up that lined the faded and worn boardwalk in front of the store.

Verne walked into the store and let the rickety wooden screen door slam behind him. He glanced around for any sign of life but found none.

"Hey! Pete!" he shouted. There was no reply. He walked up to the counter, leaned across, and looked behind it, as though someone might be hiding there. The space behind the counter was empty. Verne listened but heard only the sound of the spinning fan blades above him and an unrecognizable country music song playing somewhere off in the distance.

"Pete! You here?" He listened again and immediately recognized the cowboy boot shuffling coming toward him from the back of the store. A moment later, he saw Pete come around a corner and lumber up the aisle toward him. "Could hear those boots from a mile away, Pete. You sure those are the right size for you?"

Pete smiled. "Yep."

Verne, with his hands in his pockets, looked at Pete, expecting more.

"Verne," Pete said.

"Pete," Verne replied. "You okay?"

"Oh fine, just fine, Verne. I was just in the back, lettin' go of the morning biscuits and gravy, if ya know what I mean. Yeah, I shouldn't eat 'em, but sometimes I just can't say no. Went right through me like the Yellowstone River in June."

"Thanks for sharing," Verne said.

Pete grinned and pulled his pants higher and over his distended gut. He adjusted the dirty ball cap on his head. "What can I do for ya today, Verne?"

"I need some supplies. I thought I would head out to the hunting cabin for a while. It sits out there in the middle of nowhere all by its lonesome for all but a week or two every year, and I thought I'd get some use out of it."

"How long ya goin' for?"

"A month or two . . . or three," Verne said.

Pete looked at him quizzically.

Verne wondered if Pete had read the morning paper but assumed he had not. Pete didn't seem to care much about what went on outside his store. His only connections to the outside world were the people who walked through the front door and the phone, which sat on his desk behind the counter and only handled incoming calls. It was early enough in the morning that the possibility of the news infiltrating Pete's world was slim.

"What the hell you gonna do out there for two months?" Pete said. "Ya know I ain't got no porno here to keep you busy for that long." Pete chuckled to himself in a way that made his belly jiggle.

"Pete, you know all those books I've been asking you to get for me?"

"Sure."

"Well, they seem to be stacking up and getting a bit out of control. I need to catch up. I thought I'd throw a few boxes into the truck and make a vacation out of it."

Pete looked at Verne as if he was from another planet. "A *readin'* vacation? Is that what ya said?"

"Of course, I'll bring my rifle and a fly rod to help fill the hours." That seemed to settle a little better with Pete.

"So, you're goin' out to the hunting cabin to hunt and to fish?"

"Of course," Verne said.

"Well, let's get ya set then," Pete said. "Grab that big cart, and I'll make the rounds with ya."

Verne grabbed the metal handle of the four-by-six, sided flatbed and wheeled it behind him, following Pete down the first aisle.

"Buddy goin' with ya?" Pete asked.

"Won't go anywhere without him. Make sure you give me the good stuff for him."

Pete loaded the bags of kibble into the cart, and Verne followed him around, aisle by aisle, throwing items into the cart without much thought of cost or preference. He simply needed everything, and everything is what he picked.

It took three full carts and three trips to the truck before Verne felt comfortable that he had all he needed. He let Buddy out of the cab and brought him inside the store to wait, about half an hour, while Pete put his mental calculator to the test and added up the bill.

Verne paid the bill with cash, which always made Pete happy. "Thanks, Pete. It's been a pleasure as always."

"Pleasure's all mine," Pete said as he pocketed the money.

They shook hands and smiled at each other.

"Till next time," Pete said.

"Until the next time," Verne replied. It was their way of saying goodbye without having to say goodbye, a tradition Pete started the first time Verne met him. Verne turned and headed for the door, and Buddy followed.

"Verne?" Pete said.

Verne turned around. "Yeah, Pete?"

"You be all right out there, by yourself and all, no connection to the rest of the world?"

"I've got Buddy," Verne said.

"Ain't as young as ya used to be. What if ya need somethin'?"

"We'll be fine, but thanks." Verne pushed the screen door open and held it so Buddy could run through the doorway.

"Verne?"

Verne turned back again. "Yeah, Pete?"

"Could come by every couple weeks or so, if ya like."

Verne knew Pete well and knew there was only one way this parting would ever actually happen. "Sure, Pete. That would be great. But only if you have the time, and if you can't, I'll understand."

Pete smiled. "See ya in a couple."

Verne nodded and walked out. As he pulled away, he glanced back and saw Pete in the doorway, his nose pressed against the screen of the door as he waved.

For Verne, the first week at the cabin was a time of transition, of settling in. He had been alone for some time now, since the passing of his wife, but being out at the hunting cabin was a different form of solitary confinement. On past visits, he had come out with his buddies from the local VFW, but this was the first time he had come alone. Aside from Buddy, all he had for companionship were the birds, the whitetail deer, and the dozens of other creatures that made this particular slice of heaven their home.

His cabin was simple and efficient. The logs that made up the four walls had been felled more than a hundred years ago, and it seemed that the mud that filled the gaps between the logs had come from an ancient riverbed. The tin roof was red with rust, and a slender river rock chimney protruded through it at one corner. A small, covered porch hung off the front of the cabin, the perfect place from which to gaze at the towering pines that rose up the slope of the bluff just across the dirt road. Inside, there was a single room that had a bed, two high-back chairs covered in cracked and worn leather, a small wooden table with three chairs, and a fireplace. He would cook by fire, get his water from the nearby creek, and take care of his daily business in the confines of the great outdoors.

After Verne picked up his supplies from Pete's, he had gone home to pick up three boxes of additional necessities. Two of the boxes contained books. The third box was filled with bourbon. Now in the cabin, the books were out of their boxes and dispersed all around. Verne wanted them laid out so that no matter what direction he might glance, he would see a book there to catch his attention. The box of bourbon was in the corner, two bottles lighter than when it first arrived. His cabin was perfect.

It wasn't long before Verne settled into a routine. He was up at dawn every morning with the first sound of the birds. He and Buddy would walk for a good hour through the surrounding forest, each of them looking around for something, anything of interest, and always listening. Sometimes they would head for the nearby creek, other times for the valley where they could always find some white-tails grazing in the dew-laden grasses. At the creek, Verne would fish while Buddy chased hidden critters up and down the banks. If Verne didn't have his fly rod, he had his shotgun in tow, always ready to pick off a game bird from the sky. Back at the cabin, Verne would have his coffee and read for a few hours before breaking for lunch, which usually consisted of something simple and easy to prepare, like a can of soup and a glass of water. After lunch, he napped for an hour and then he was back to his books for the remainder of the afternoon. He started to think about having a drink at four but always held off until six, as he found he could not remember what he read while the bourbon was flowing through his veins. At six, he would pour a tumbler full and get dinner started. At eight, with the dinner dishes washed and put away, he would sit at the table and write in his journal for as long as the words flowed from his brain to his pen to the paper. For his journal writing, the bourbon was a grand facilitator, opening up the neural paths and manipulating connections both typical and unique. At nine, he was out on the porch sitting in an antique rocking chair with Buddy lying at his feet. He would wear his wool jacket to fend off the cool air that came with the dusk, and he would settle into a quiet evening with a second tumbler of bourbon and a pack of Lucky Strike cigarettes. He would sip, smoke, and listen to the endless sounds of nature until his eyelids became heavy and finally closed of their own free will. At the first sound of a rumbling snore, Buddy would get up and nudge Verne awake, and they would go into the cabin for a good night's rest.

Verne was living a life of wished-for solitude; a dream realized. For so many years throughout his career, Verne often thought about the possibility of getting away from it all, from the many distractions that diverted him from what he most cared about. His wife had always put his dreams and his wishes into perspective, providing a view of reality encumbered by the arguable variables of work and family and all the rest. She assured him that there would always be something important that would keep him tied to his well-known and well-lived life: another election, local investments, friends and family, and future grandchildren.

He thought about his wife often, and late one evening in the middle of the eighth week, he received an unexpected visit from her, in a dream. Before going to sleep, Verne had hit the bottle a little more heavily than usual, for no particular reason other than that the bourbon was going down good and his mind was racing. The more he thought about things, the more he drank, and the more he drank, the more his mind reached for explanations, for answers. As usual, he ended up falling asleep on the front porch, but Buddy was unsuccessful at rousing him from his alcohol-induced slumber. He awoke with a chill at the earliest moments of dawn, stumbled inside, and crawled under the covers as Buddy settled in on a braided rug at the foot of the bed. After just an hour more of sleep, the dream came to him, causing him to bolt upright. His heart raced as sweat glistened on his forehead. He got out of bed, started a fire, and hung the coffee pot over it. His heart calmed with the percolating beat. He poured a couple fingers of bourbon and sat before the fire, aching for a feeling of warmth that was long in coming.

The next day, his typical daily schedule was disrupted, for he could not shake the dream. He didn't leave the cabin, he didn't read, and a mid-day nap was not an option. The dream haunted him. He ate little throughout the day and was not surprised that his first evening sip had an immediate, almost hallucinatory effect. He spent the evening on the porch, drinking and smoking and not thinking about the dream but instead considering what might have prompted it in the first place. Verne had led a long and interesting life, one that other people would consider successful. However, a significant number of Verne's choices in life came with baggage—not just consequences, but heavy baggage and lots of it. Verne thought about some of those choices as he rocked in his chair, and he wondered if it had all been worth it. All the ties to his past life were no longer in place. His career was over and he had ended his life as a public servant on a positive note, but there were skeletons in his career closet. Most of his old buddies were either dead or in Florida, waiting to die. The neighborhood had turned over twice since he and his wife first moved in and the current inhabitants were barely acquaintances. He had liquidated his local investments years back, and the correlating memories were already vague and distant. His wife was dead, and late one evening a long, long time ago, a driver likely distracted by something electronic and surely less important than life itself had taken his only child from this world, a lifetime too soon.

He wondered about how he had gotten to this place, to this time. Was it simply fate, or life itself, that had steered him to his current destination? Was he the navigator? Did he have a hand in how his life turned out, or was he simply a puppet dangling from strings manipulated by a much higher power? Did the choices he made, right or wrong, have an negative impact on the people he loved? Did the endless and relentless media inquiries and the resulting public communications tarnish what would have otherwise been a burnished life? The questions came quickly and steadily, but the answers evaded him. He racked his brain into the early hours of the morning until, distraught and frustrated, he went inside to go to sleep. He was fortunate that his wife returned to him once again while he slept, and he awoke late in the morning to a freshly risen sun, a steady heat, and the realization that everything was going to be all right. His wife had told him so.

It was on a beautiful and crisp morning at the end of his tenth week at the cabin that Verne felt that something was wrong. Just like that last day in town, some age-worn instinct had put him on alert. Pete had not shown up for his last visit and at first, Verne did not think anything of it. He assumed something had come up or simply that Pete had lost interest. That was two weeks ago. Now, Verne was not so sure. As he sat out on the front porch and listened to the birds and the wind, he sensed something was different. He wondered if maybe all the solitude was getting to him. Maybe the books and the visions were trying to tell him something. Maybe the bourbon was. He couldn't put his finger on what exactly was troubling him, but there was an uncomfortable knot in his stomach that he couldn't shake. Verne, as a politician, had a history of following his gut, and his gut was telling him something was wrong, terribly wrong. His gut was telling him to go back into town.

Within an hour, Verne had the truck packed, the cabin locked up, and Buddy was in the front seat waiting for him. He looked around one last time, said goodbye to the cabin, hopped into the truck with Buddy, and drove away. It seemed to Verne that he could not drive fast enough to settle his anxiety, but he eased up on the accelerator when Buddy started to whimper.

He felt the need to get into town quickly, but Pete's store was coming up on the left. He turned in and pulled up to the building with locked brakes, the tires skidding across the pebbled drive. He hurried inside and stood at the front counter, just as he had done ten weeks earlier.

"Hey, Pete!" he shouted. "Pete!"

He heard nothing except the same spinning fan blades and the radio in the distance. Only the song had changed. He looked around, and the store looked as it always did. He eyed the desk and saw that it was a mess as usual, but something was different. He thought about what he was seeing and realized that the desktop had a new inhabitant—new to the desk, but old to the world. Sitting at the far corner of the desk was an old computer, covered in dust. In fact, Verne quickly realized that most of the desk and the things on top of it were covered in dust, which he thought was odd. He looked down at the countertop in front of him and saw a fine coating of dust there as well. Verne considered the countertop curiously, as he used his index finger to write in the dust, "Verne was here."

He hurried back to the truck, quickly got back onto Route 89, and headed north into town. The two-lane highway was deserted, which was always possible depending on the time of day, but at nine o'clock on a Friday morning, it seemed to Verne that there should be someone out and about on his way to work or school or fishing.

There was no one.

As he entered the town limits, the wind howled through the

many drafty, broken seals of his truck and moved with such a force as to nudge his truck across the center yellow line. He grabbed the wheel with both hands and slowed the truck as he looked with amazement at the snow-like particles floating through the air. Verne had seen his share of unusual weather in his six years in Montana, and had even experienced a snowstorm, hail, heavy rain, and seventy-degree sunshine in the same day, but he had never seen snow in July. He squinted through the windshield and examined the floating flakes, noticed their gray tint, and quickly realized that what was falling from the sky was not snow at all. He turned on the windshield wipers to swipe away the accumulating dust.

He continued down Main Street, driving well below the speed limit and not worrying if there might be someone behind him. He was taking it all in, trying to make sense of what he was seeing. Cars lined the streets as usual, but most had their doors open. All the storefronts were dark, and it was eerily silent. He rolled down his window just a crack and listened. All he could hear was the wind and the sound of his heart beating in his ears.

Verne pulled up in front of the diner and parked. He looked through his dusty windshield at the lifeless façade and stepped out of the truck. He hurried inside, but once there realized there was no need to hurry. The diner was dark and empty, with every surface covered in dust. He walked behind the counter and looked around. Aside from the dust, everything seemed in order. He stepped up to the cash register and pressed a button. The drawer slid out, revealing a full till loaded with cash and coins. He closed the drawer and slid his hand along the underside of the counter, found what he was looking for, and gently pulled it from its holster. Anyone who knew Bob Harrison, the proprietor, knew about the palm-sized .22 caliber revolver he kept behind the counter. Bob would often say, more loudly than necessary, "In case anyone gets out of line or criticizes the cook." Then he would show the backside of his hand, wait a second, and turn his hand around to show the revolver resting in his palm. He would raise his eyebrows and flash a smirk, which always roused a round of applause from someone. Verne thought about Bob's regular event, and it made him smile. He pocketed the gun and grabbed the box of ammunition on the shelf below. He left the diner in an unusual manner—he did not say goodbye.

He drove around the quiet and dusty streets of town for a few minutes and realized there was no point in driving or searching any further. His town was a ghost town if there ever was one. He headed back out onto Main Street, got back onto Route 89, and drove out of town with a heavy foot.

Verne was forty or so miles outside of town when he spotted a dark, moving dot far in the distance. His mind raced through the possibilities, but before he could deduce the correct result, he was able to make out a vehicle racing toward him. His heart quickened, and he tightened his grip on the wheel. It seemed like an eternity to him, but just ten seconds later, a black pickup truck passed him on the left. He glued his eyes to the rearview mirror to get a sight on it as it continued down the road. At a distance of about a hundred yards, Verne saw the truck's red brake lights glow and watched the truck pull off to the side of the road. Verne slowed his truck while keeping an eye on the road in front of him as he veered off to the shoulder. He gazed into the rearview mirror for a long time, staring at the pickup behind him in the distance. Both trucks remained motionless, engines idling.

Verne took his eyes off the mirror for just a moment to look forward, and that is when he heard the sound of screeching tires. His head snapped around, and he turned to watch through the back window as the black pickup truck approached. At a hundred feet, the truck pulled over again, stopped, and waited. Verne looked through the back window and into the bed of his truck and saw his shotgun lying there in its case, close but impossible to reach. He groped at his front pocket, and his heart calmed some as he felt Bob's revolver. He looked up from the bed to the pickup truck behind him and watched as the driver's-side door opened. A young, dark-haired woman stepped out of the truck and stood next to it, slowly raising her hands to show empty palms. Verne turned around, stared at the steering wheel, and thought about his next move. There wasn't much to think about, so he opened the door and stepped out. He turned back to Buddy. "You stay right there, boy."

"I'm not armed," the young woman yelled. Before Verne could say anything, she added, "Let me see your hands!"

Verne slowly raised both hands. "Take it easy, young lady. I mean you no harm."

They stared at each other for a long minute. Then the young woman started to walk toward him. Verne lifted the collar of his coat to deflect the breeze and put his hands into his front pockets. His right hand slid easily over the revolver, and he took comfort in feeling the cold steel of the barrel. He walked slowly toward her.

"You come from town?" she asked.

"Yeah," Verne said. "There's no town left."

"Figured as much," she said. "But I was holding out hope."

"There's no hope there either."

They were fifty feet from each other and the gap was closing.

"Where'd you come from, before that?" she asked.

"I've been out at my hunting cabin for the last ten weeks, away from everything. It seems like I missed out on something."

"You could say that," the young woman said.

At twenty feet, Verne watched as the young woman reached behind and pulled an automatic handgun from her belt. He watched her fearless eyes and her smooth confidence as she swung the gun around and raised it level to his chest. His grip tightened on the revolver in his pocket, but he did not flinch and continued to walk toward her.

"That's far enough," she said.

"There's no need for that," Verne said, motioning with his head toward her gun.

"A girl can't be too careful these days, *especially* these days."

"I'm just an old man, trying to figure out what the hell is going on."

"Hell indeed," she said.

Verne did not follow what she meant. He stopped and stared at her.

She slowly lowered her gun and stuck it in the front of her jeans. "You're not that old," she said as she cracked the slightest of smiles.

Verne's grip on the revolver in his pocket loosened. He pulled out both hands to show that they were empty and said, "I'm harmless. I just want to find out what's going on."

The young woman walked closer. She stopped two feet from him, pulled a pack of cigarettes from the inside pocket of her leather jacket and in doing so, revealed a young and fit upper body concealed by only a thin, white t-shirt. Verne noticed, and the young woman noticed him noticing. She pulled a cigarette from the pack and lit it. "Smoke?" she asked.

"Why not," Verne replied.

She handed him a cigarette and stepped forward to light it. It was the first time a woman had ever offered to light a cigarette for him. He smiled. As she held the flame, Verne leaned in and drew deep on the cigarette. He exhaled slowly and smacked his lips for the flavor.

"You're very kind," Verne said.

"Been away ten weeks, huh? Why should I believe you?"

Verne shrugged. "Are you going to tell me what's going on?"

The young woman took a drag and pondered the question. "You first."

"There's not much to tell," Verne said. "I packed up my truck and my dog ten weeks ago and headed out to my hunting cabin for a little rest and relaxation. This morning, I woke up and felt the urge to drive into town. Found a lot of nothing . . . except for all the dust."

The young woman stared at him. Verne remained quiet.

"That's it?"

"That's it," Verne said. "Now it's your turn."

She took another long drag, then dropped the cigarette and stubbed it out on the pavement with her boot. "Went on a camping trip with my boyfriend a week ago. We were in the park, having a good old time, and then he started to get restless. Yeah, once the beer ran out, he got fidgety. So, last night he left me at the campsite and headed for town, the bastard. Said he'd be back in an hour or so, but I knew better. It'd be an easy two hours, assuming he didn't stop for a few cold ones, which I knew he would. At eleven o'clock last night, he still wasn't back, so I went to sleep. I woke up this morning, and I knew something was wrong. I could *feel* it. The world didn't sound right, and the clouds that floated by in the sky were unlike any clouds I'd ever seen before."

She reached for another cigarette and lit it.

"Those weren't clouds," Verne said.

"I know."

"What the hell happened?" Verne tried again.

She tensed a bit but took a couple drags and calmed herself. "I usually take a shortwave radio with me whenever I'm traveling. It's something I picked up from my granddad. I always felt better knowing that I could hear somebody, anybody, no matter where I was. So this morning, I got a report out of New York, some guy saying something went wrong, terribly wrong, with the country's communication systems. It's hard to believe." She paused. "Impossible to believe."

Verne rubbed his chin, feeling the two-day-old whiskers. "Young lady, what in God's name are you talking about?"

The young woman started to cry. "They're all gone."

"What?"

"Everybody . . . gone."

"Come on. I've had a rough couple of days. Come clean."

The young woman stopped crying in mid sniffle. "Listen, I'm no rocket scientist, but I'm no idiot either. I was listening to the Emergency Broadcast System. You know of it?"

"Sure."

"They said to stay away from any and all communications equipment. Reports I've been hearing from those that are left, *out there*, is that anyone within close proximity to any communications device at eleven-thirty last night was exposed to a level of radiation unheard of in modern times." She started to cry again. "My poor Billy. Gone."

Verne did not know what to say, or what to do. He wondered why anyone would be using a shortwave radio given what had supposedly happened, but he lost the thought quickly. He stood and continued to draw from his cigarette, even though the ember was burning the filter. He watched the young woman closely.

After a minute, she stopped crying and collected herself; her time of mourning appeared to stop as quickly as it had started. "Radiation—communications equipment—you think it's possible?"

"Young lady, I was a politician. Anything's possible."

She processed the response and accepted the possibility. "So, it's just you and me," she said.

"And the shortwave people," Verne added.

She nodded. "Well, it's been fun, but I must be moving along."

"Me too," Verne said, and wondered to where he might be moving along.

"Where'd you say your hunting cabin was?" she asked.

"I didn't say."

"Right," she said. She turned and walked back toward her truck.

"You got a name?" Verne yelled.

She turned around. "Marion. You?"

"Verne."

She smiled. "Verne, it's been a pleasure. I'll be up in the park for a few days until things settle down, so I can get my act together." She turned and walked back to her truck. She pulled onto the road and drove toward him, then slowed and stopped alongside where he was standing. Through the passenger window she said, "Until next time."

Verne smiled and nodded. "Until next time."

The young woman sped away and disappeared into the distance.

Verne pulled the pack of Lucky Strike cigarettes from his shirt pocket and lit one. "Hey, Buddy. Come here." Buddy lunged from the driver's seat of the truck and sprinted toward him. Verne leaned down and rubbed the dog on the top of his head. "Good boy." They walked back toward the truck, slowly, giving him time to finish his cigarette.

Just a few feet from the truck, Verne stopped, and Buddy stopped alongside him. Verne looked up into the sky and watched the dust clouds float by. For some reason, he thought about Ted back at the office of the town newspaper, on the phone and getting the latest scoop. Verne envisioned Ted's unlikely demise, and that made him smile.

NOTES ON
COME OUT, WHEREVER YOU ARE

These days, our world is enmeshed in technological connectivity—twenty-four hours a day, seven days a week. Internet services and social network capabilities available to the individual are endless, and as a result, many people spend the majority of their days searching and texting and updating their networks of people on every minute detail of their existence. Time that used to be spent reading and thinking or just doing nothing is now filled with a seemingly endless stream of digital communications. What is everyone communicating about? In addition, anything (and everything!) a person may say or do can be captured instantly by one of the millions of smartphone devices lurking around every corner. The thought is unnerving. Personal privacy is an afterthought and is most certainly in jeopardy. Not only that, but we're at risk of losing our individual identities in a sea of social media consumption.

Don't get me wrong; I like technology as much as the next person. I realize that our current technologies and communication capabilities are endless and can prove to be tremendously beneficial, but where does it all end? Is it possible to be too consumed and too connected? I think so.

I think we need to be forced away from our devices every once in a while to relish the simple pleasures in life: reading a book, taking a walk, or just looking around and taking in all that is happening around us. For without the break, we might get so distracted that we'll miss out on what is really important.

What if a person decided to walk away from the technological tether and live his life in solitude, and what if while he was away, the social network imploded and took its membership with it? That, very simply, was the seed of the idea, and it was all I needed to get on with writing *Come Out, Wherever You Are*.

In the story, the protagonist, Verne, had forced himself to break away. During his career as a politician, he was always in the spotlight and always in the news. Privacy was not a possibility and he understood that the absence of it came with the job. So, as he came to the end of his career, he made a wish and then when he retired, he made the wish a reality. What he didn't expect was for the circumstances that nudged him into exile to end up being the same circumstances that made his exile permanent. Sometimes, we have to be careful what we wish for.

When I sat down to write the story, I had the beginning and the ending in mind. In most cases, it is a necessity for me. I need to visualize the opening scene and have some idea of how the story will end. I need the final bit of action or the final sentence. With those basic story components solidified, only then am I able to effectively set out on the journey to reach that ending.

Coming up with a main character—someone struggling with technology—was easy. Politicians, more than anyone, need technology to further their cause. At the same time, technology can ruin a career, a person. If you're a politician, the technology and the person behind it is always there—always in your face—to help or hurt you. It's a true Catch-22 situation.

So, I had the main character, and I knew exactly where to put him. I fell in love with Montana on my first visit there over ten years ago, and I have been pursuing my own temporary but regular exile in that state ever since. The sky is big, the rivers are endless, and I think the people there are likely the nicest people in the world. Add to that—regarding the people, there are only about one million in the entire state. There is one square mile of land for every six people. It's open and easy to get lost there, and I like the possibilities. Montana was where Verne needed to go.

I knew Verne would start and end his story in Montana, and after the fateful technology-induced demise of the human race, I expected him to simply head off into the sunset to finish out his remaining years in solitude, as he had wished. What I didn't expect was the response I received from initial readers and editors with whom I shared the story. Most everyone wanted to know what happened next. Two people very specifically noted that the story read like the first chapter of a novel, as if it was just getting started, and I found that interesting. When I finished writing the story there was no more; I had no more. Verne got what he ultimately wanted, and that was that. But since that time, I have given the comments I received a little more thought and find that I'm often wondering— maybe even worrying—about Verne and what his future holds. Who knows, maybe I will run into him again somewhere down the road.

This past summer, I had the fortunate opportunity to join our Boy Scout troop on a 100-mile backpacking adventure in northern New Mexico. On the day we arrived at base camp, I collected everyone's smartphones and locked them away, as no electronics were allowed for the ten days on the trail. There was a little complaining, but most everyone conceded willingly. At the time, I could only imagine what was going to happen to these nine very connected people in our crew, myself included. Would everyone freak out from technology withdrawal? Surprisingly, the devices were a distant memory just an hour later. It happened that fast. And without the devices, the most amazing thing happened: everyone looked around and took in the sights and talked to one another.

I hope we figure out how to create an appropriate balance between life and technology. I hold out great hope, but until we do, let us all be careful of what we wish for. And, by the way, watch out for that device next to you.

At the End of the Day

I'd seen those eyes a thousand times since we first met five years ago and had looked into them for inspiration, support, and guidance, but today I saw in her blue-dotted pearls something different, and what I saw stirred in me something that I had never quite felt before.

The morning proceeded according to plan, without a hitch and much like the mornings of the past two weeks. I had the same rushed breakfast at the hotel and hurried cab ride, walked into the same indistinguishable studio, and met the producer and the pleasant and somewhat interested interviewer (albeit only interested in the potential ratings boost). I heard the same questions, gave mostly the same answers, and then I heard, "We're out," from someone standing off in the distance, giving me a momentary break. The network provided a comfortable room down the hall from the studio where I could decompress with a drink and some fresh fruit before heading out for the final event of the publicity tour this evening.

My new film, which hits theaters tomorrow through a highly anticipated national release, is an engaging and unique crime drama penned by an up-and-coming screenwriter I know from the old days in Chicago. He said he wrote the film with me in mind for the lead

33

role, which I believed when I read the script. I've been making films now for ten years, and sometimes when you read a script, you know you're going to do the film for the money. On rare occasions, as I experienced with this film, I knew I was going to make it because the story was good, because the story meant something. Even though I might not be able to explain what that something is, I don't care because I *feel* it.

The publicity tour is part of the filmmaking process. You can spend two months or two years working on a film, but it's the two weeks before the release that determines whether the gross is twenty million or a hundred million. I've never questioned the schedule or the motives of the studio, and I try to make every appearance and every interview somewhat meaningful for the moviegoer. It's a bitch, cramming forty events into a two-week period, but then it's over. I go to the movie premiere, the studio releases the film, then it's out of my hands and time for me to move on.

Jen was sitting on a hardback chair, which she turned around so she could rest her arms up on the back, with her chin resting on her wrists. She faced me and sat a bit higher than where I was on the couch. She was looking at me with eyebrows raised and an enchanting smile.

"What?" I asked.

"That was a good interview—the best one yet," she said.

"You think? She did seem to be a little more interested than the rest. Maybe it was because we started a little later, and there was time for the caffeine to kick in."

"I think she likes you. She said she was a fan, that she had seen all your movies."

"She's a good interviewer," I said, "but not really my type."

Jen continued smiling.

"What?" I asked.

"They're all your type," she said.

Jen has been my publicist for five years now. She knows me. It wasn't always that way, and I guess I am a little surprised at how our relationship has evolved. A friend of a friend referred her to me, and while she had excellent credentials, I was initially concerned about her age. She was a good twenty years older than my previous publicist, who had left me for a husband and a little one on the way. She is almost twenty years older than I am. But when I met her that first time in my office and saw her youthful skin and toned body, her fifty-three years looked more like forty-three, which pared the difference down to eight years, and from that moment on, age was never an issue. She had maturity, experience, and perspective, coupled with youth in her heart, and she had a passion for life. I liked that. I still do.

At first, our relationship was all business. Her job was to get me in front of the moviegoer. It took her a while to get started, and at first, I thought it was because she was settling in, learning the process, and learning about me. It was likely those things, but I also knew she had recently gone through a tough time. I had asked the friend of my friend about her, as part of the hiring process, and learned that she had lost her husband to cancer. Sometimes, in the years since I met Jen, I have wondered about my career in the entertainment business and what the point is, especially when there is so much pain in the world. All I can come up with is that maybe, just maybe, I can provide some reprieve, can give someone a couple of hours to leave the world behind and get lost in another story, in another world. Jen was good at keeping her grief from me, and in five years, she has never said a word about it. I never told her that I knew. It didn't matter.

I realized later that her approach was to learn as much about me as she could, for only then could she effectively sell me and my story to a potential audience. It took four months for her to book my first publicity event, but the event resulted in media coverage for a week and I have never questioned her approach since. She cares about my career. That much I know for certain, and what in this life is ever certain?

"They're not all my type," I said, defending myself. "I've refined my tastes over the years."

"Yeah, very refined," she said. She smiled, which made her squint, and the light from above flashed as a sparkle in the corner of her right eye.

As I said, I saw something different in her eyes. My first reaction was concern, but that feeling passed. I felt that she wanted to say something—something important, meaningful. I kept my mouth shut and just looked at her, looked deep into those beautiful and caring eyes, and wondered what she might be thinking. I heard my anxious stomach groan and hoped she could not hear.

I wanted to say something to him, but I just wasn't sure it was the right time. Is there ever a right time? The much-younger version of me would have just said it; whatever was on my mind would have come out without any hesitation whatsoever. I used to "tell it like it is," and usually could do it tactfully and without getting myself into trouble. I used to put it all out there—my feelings—without regard for the consequences. I lived life on a whim, and used to live, and love, in the moment. When my husband died six years ago, that all changed. I gave myself to him. Everything I had was on the line, every feeling and emotion was exposed and committed to our relationship, and then in the blur of one month, everything I was living for was gone.

I quit my job and spent the next year trying to forget. I packed up everything of his in the house and gave it away. I thought I needed to erase any physical reminder of him, as the mental reminders would be enough to carry me forward, or torture me, for years to come. I was wrong. When the house finally sold, that last reminder passed off to a young couple not very different than we had been ten years earlier, I realized I had made a mistake. For the following nine months, I sat alone in a mostly empty apartment in the city, and I tried to remember him, all the good times we had and all the love we shared, but I couldn't. I wished I had kept something, anything, as a totem to keep me connected to him. All I could remember was the smoothness of his scalp and the ashen, gaunt face and the emptiness of his yellow eyes. That image still haunts me, but now I see a smile on his lips and can sometimes hear him whispering to move on.

There was a year of mourning and self-pity, and it was my friend Karen who finally stepped in to help me get back on my feet. After a month-long reintroduction to the world, she referred me to a friend of hers who was looking for a publicist. That's what I had done in my previous life, and I wondered if I could be good at it again. I tried to question myself, but Karen would have none of it. She set the date for the interview, took me shopping for some new clothes, and spent three evenings over dinner and wine, grilling me endlessly to prepare me for the interview. It wasn't until the morning of the interview that she told me I would be meeting with a popular and successful actor who was also one of the world's most eligible bachelors.

For five years now, I have committed myself to Jeremy's career. It's been a good five years, and he's a great guy to work for. He makes good movies and makes it easy for me to share him with the world. The fact that I am older than he is has proven to be beneficial, for both of us. I've been around a bit and have learned how to distinguish the fake from the genuine. I can be protective, like a mother, while still letting him push up against the boundaries of life's challenges. He has asked me for my advice on a wide range of topics and issues, both professional and personal, and, given my situation and perspective, I have never held back. He is young and successful and can have any woman he wants, and I have been fortunate not to be caught up in his personal life when it comes to other women—that is, until now.

Jeremy had just finished his last interview for the planned publicity tour, and I was sitting across from him, not wanting to talk about the interview the way we had talked about all the others by reviewing the questions, answers, and possible media interpretations. We had come to the end, and I wanted it to be different this time. As I was thinking about what to say next, he sat across from me with his legs crossed and his hands folded in his lap. He had a boyish grin on his face, and he was staring at me, waiting for me to speak.

It didn't feel like the right time.

"So you're free until later this afternoon," I said. "The premiere is at eight, and you need to be in your suite, ready for makeup and wardrobe at four. I'll have a car pick up Samantha, and she will arrive at the hotel at five. I've reserved a private cubby for you at The Club Room, and Samantha's favorite flowers will be on the table as you requested. Dinner is from five-thirty to seven, and then you'll head over to the theater."

"Thank you," he said, and continued to stare.

I looked at him and watched his grin grow into a full, pearly-white smile. "What are you looking at, uh, smiling about?" I asked.

"Nothing, nothing at all. You have taken care of everything, as always."

I watched his smile fade and his expression turn more serious. He chewed his bottom lip, and I could tell that something else was on his mind. I said, "I'll be there with you on the red carpet and will coordinate all the press activities. Just follow my lead."

"Of course," he said.

"Okay then," I said. "The car should be waiting for us downstairs."

He did not say anything, but he sat and smiled again.

"Is everything all right?" I asked.

"Fine. Is there anything else you want to talk about? Anything else you want to ask me?" His eyebrows inched up on his forehead.

"No, that's it," I said.

We sat and looked at each other, and I couldn't help but smile back at him. He has that way with me.

His phone rang. As he reached to pull the phone from his pocket, he said, "Why don't we get together this afternoon for some . . ." He cut himself off and answered the call.

Get together this afternoon, for some . . . What was he saying? My heart quickened.

He listened intently, and his smile faded. After a minute of nodding with sincere interest, he said, "Samantha, dear, don't worry about it. You just stay home and take care of yourself. I'll call you later to see how you're doing." He hung up.

"Is everything okay?" I asked.

"Samantha has come down with the flu, the poor thing. She sounds terrible. Her friend Keri is there with her, making sure she's well taken care of."

"I'll get right on it. I'll have another date for you within the hour," I said.

His smile returned. "Would you go with me as my date?" he asked.

I would likely have fallen to the floor if I didn't have the back of the chair to hold onto. "Don't be silly. I've got work to do when I'm there. I can't be holding onto your arm as well."

"I'm going to have to insist. I don't want to be worrying the rest of the afternoon about who you're going to set me up with." He chewed his lip again. "I'm going to have to pull rank on you. I'm the boss, right?"

"You're the boss," I said.

"Then it's settled. You'll be my date this evening, and I'll see you at five-thirty for dinner." He smiled, rose from his chair, and headed for the exit. "C'mon, our car is waiting."

What could I do? This was his big day, and who was I to go against the boss's wishes? I smiled, and as my cheeks pushed up and made me squint, I sensed that a tear duct had relaxed some and glazed my right eye.

I hoped he didn't notice.

DAY 8

When I asked Jen to join me for the premiere of my movie, it seemed like a natural thing to do. To be perfectly honest, all I knew was that I wanted to spend the evening with her and wanted to share the excitement and spectacle. I didn't want her to direct the evening and protect me from the media. I wanted to do the directing and pro-tecting. The thought of having her on my arm as I walked the red carpet just seemed right, and I didn't care or think about anything else. It was probably good that I didn't.

We had a great time, but there were some repercussions to deal with the next day. The media was relentless, and I spent most of the morning ignoring inquiries about my personal life. They didn't need to hear from me. No matter what I might say, they would go ahead and print whatever they felt would create the best story. The one call I could not ignore came from Samantha, still sick and absolutely furious. I tried to calm her and assure her that my time with Jen was purely professional, but I knew Samantha well and realized it was the beginning of the end.

The week after the premiere flew by like a blur. The movie premiere generated all the publicity we had hoped for and then some, thanks to Jen. The first-day sales for the national theater release were higher than those for any of my previous movies, and the weekend gross hit forty million, well above the studio's expectation. Everyone was happy; everyone, that is, but Samantha. She ended our relationship, if you could call it that, just two days into the post-premiere media frenzy. She said she wanted a commitment, and she felt I was incapable of making such a pledge. I don't know if she's right. It's just not something I spend time thinking about. She felt that I had betrayed her, which I thought was silly. Maybe I had, and I just didn't know it at the time.

It took a little coercing, but Jen agreed to have dinner with me later in the week. It was a dinner unlike any I had experienced before, and only one part of a night I could not have imagined. We drank wine, enjoyed a fabulous meal, and talked for hours while sharing a couple of desserts. In the five years we had worked together, we had never grown so personal. We let our guards down and talked about what was on our minds, about what was real. I took her home and walked her to her door, and she kissed me on the cheek. It was the softest, most tender kiss, like a butterfly brushing its wings on a leaf. I went home with my mind reeling, feeling like a teenager after a first date.

The next day we spent the afternoon at the art museum, and she shared with me everything she knew about Pierre-Auguste Renoir. She taught me that he was a leader in the development of the Impressionist style—a fact I likely should have known—and showed me her favorite paintings and sketches. She's so real, so genuine, that I'm not sure I can measure up. We went back to my place and ordered a pizza. We drank a great bottle of wine and listened to music that spanned three decades. As the evening ended and I went to get our coats, she said we wouldn't need them, not until morning.

I feel like I'm caught up in a whirlwind with a man whom I know quite well, and yet I don't really know him at all. I'm not sure what happened a week ago as I sat across from him after his last interview, but I knew I wanted to leave the past behind, as best I could, and make an effort to move forward, to live again and to love again. I had a whole speech planned for him, but I never got to use it. Life, maybe even fate, intervened. Samantha got sick, Jeremy invited me to join him at the premiere, and here I am a week later, spinning. I've had the most enjoyable week I could ever imagine, and life seems to mean something for me again. It seems to mean something for

Jeremy.

I have strong feelings about keeping my personal and professional lives separate so as not to "dip the pen in the company ink," as my husband used to say. However, I had much stronger feelings that overcame me the night I slept with Jeremy. I was at his place, sipping wine, listening to music, talking, sharing, and wasting the evening away. It all felt so right, like I could stay there with him forever, and so I stayed. I had not spent the night with a man since my husband, and Jeremy helped me through the endless hours of the night with gentle and caring affection. And did I mention passion? My God, was there passion.

Now I wonder if I've made a huge mistake. I've fallen for him. To be honest, I felt something the first time I met him, but I always knew that we were two people from two very different and quite incompatible worlds. But things changed since I went to the premier with him, and I became less concerned about what other people might think. I'm in love with him, and I feel like I'm heading down a path of no return, where the only possible outcome is pure disaster. What was I thinking? Some of my girlfriends have sons who are the same age as Jeremy. He's a movie star, for Christ's sake. What could he possibly see in me? Even if he did see something, anything, that sight would be blinded before long by the trappings of his profession. The blinding and the subsequent demise are inevitable.

DAY 74

While the movie was running its course, I decided to take two months off. I gave Jen and the rest of the staff a break as well. It's been refreshing. The last project burned me out, or maybe that was simply the best excuse I could come up with. After the opening weekend, I received several new scripts to consider, "blockbuster films," they told me, but they were all going to have to wait. My agent is pissed off, says he needs answers, but I know all he really needs is another paycheck. He'll be all right. He doesn't understand, but I have another more important project on my mind.

I have spent the last two months on a mission to become a real person. Hollywood and all that comes along with it is pure bullshit; the only reality created is a figment in the mind of some writer or producer or editor. Those of us in the acting trade are simply puppets hanging from a thousand fragile strings, pulled by the hands of a hundred different and faceless characters, who all have purely selfish motivations. I've loved my career, but I realize now, and I guess I always knew, that I was living a fantasy life. I've been living in the clouds, and now there is a beautiful, loving, and caring woman in my life who has helped to bring me back down onto solid footing.

Two months is a long time to spend on a relationship, especially when I have never given a relationship more than a few days at a time. I have done things with Jen over the last two months that I've only been able to talk about, to dream about, in the last ten years. I just never had the time. We spent a long weekend in New York and enjoyed seven plays. We ate at some new restaurants and took a long and carefree walk through Central Park, holding hands. People turned their heads and looked at us. I didn't care. Across the country on the other coast, we took long and aimless drives, learned about wine, and watched sunsets with our toes buried in the sand. I've read fifteen books, more than I've read in the last ten years, and have had an intelligent sounding board to throw my newfound ideas at. It's been the best two months of my life, and through it all, I found love—real love.

I have always had to be concerned about what others might think of my actions, as it comes with the territory. Aside from my agent, sometimes, and my publicist always, I have two people whom I can go to, eternally and with anything, and know that I'll get a rational, realistic, and always-supportive perspective, even if they don't agree with me. Those two people are my mother and my sister. My dad's not in the picture, which is fine, since he would likely call me a pussy and tell me I'm making a big mistake, just as he did when I told him I wanted to be an actor. Earlier today, I drove across town to see my sister. I told her first, for I knew she'd be the easy one to win over. She's two years younger than me and divorced, but she's a free spirit and has always lived her life doing whatever she felt she was "meant to do," as she puts it. I told her I had fallen in love with Jen, and she jumped up and down and hugged me and cried. I told her about the last two months and how what I felt for Jen was so unlike anything I had ever experienced. She could tell it was for real, and she was ecstatically happy for me. I left my sister and drove over to visit my mother, who was a bit more reserved and cautious. As she had done in the past with any hard decision I needed to make, she simply asked the questions and helped me to make sure I had all the right answers. The last question she asked was whether I was "sure" about my feelings for Jen. I told her I couldn't live without Jen, yet if I learned I couldn't spend another day with her, what we had shared over the last two months would be enough. My mother smiled. I don't know what I would do without her. She sent me on my way, with a hug and a kiss and moist eyes, and told me to go and do what I needed to do.

I just called Jen and told her I would be right over. I'm flying, head reeling and mind racing, my heart feeling like it will beat right out of my chest. I'm in love, hard-core, and I'm ready to make a commitment. I can't believe it.

I just hung up from a phone call with Jeremy. He called to let me know he was on his way over. There was something unusual about his voice, strange, but in a good way. He didn't say much, but he sounded excited. I wish I felt the same way.

My time with Jeremy has been magical. As foolish and as childish as it sounds, that is the only way I can explain it to myself. No rational explanation exists. Even after our relationship got going and the passion heated, I still never felt that I would ever truly love a man the same way I had loved my husband. It was never a possibility. After spending every day and every night over the last two months with this caring and generous young man, I learned that I was wrong.

That's what makes the situation even worse.

I got the test results back yesterday, and my most recent worst fear became a reality. Cancer. It's not like my husband's cancer, but the prognosis is about the same. The endgame is death, and the only variable is the extent and duration of the suffering. How is that possible? I cannot think about trying to get an answer, because an answer doesn't exist and it doesn't matter. Life, or fate, has stepped in again, and the sooner I accept it, the sooner I can move on.

I am most surprised at my reaction to the news. Having been through it before, I must be desensitized some. I think I may have started grieving for my husband the day we got the news about his cancer, because it had spread so fast and we both knew he didn't have a chance. And now, even though I have accepted the inevitable, it's out of my mind. I'm worried more about the person I love, and now I know how my husband must have felt. Especially in his last days, he kept telling me he didn't want to leave me, and that he didn't want to hurt me. I could see the pain deep in his eyes, and it wasn't the pain from the cancer. It was the pain of heartbreak. I feel that same pain now.

I have not slept for over twenty-four hours since I got the news. My mind and my conscience won't allow me the satisfaction. I have spent every waking moment thinking about what I should do, what I need to do. My doctor said we should start radiation right away, tomorrow. I know I should and I probably will go through with the treatments, although I have not confirmed the appointment yet. What I need to do, what I absolutely must do, is talk to Jeremy. I love Jeremy more than anything, and it is because I love him that I have to let him go. Our relationship is still fresh, still just budding, and I need to cut it off before it grows any further, although I'm not sure that's what Jeremy will ever want. All I know is that I don't want him to have to experience the loss. I have seen it and experienced it, and I wouldn't wish it on my worst enemy. I'm on my own, with few friends and even fewer family members around, and I want to keep imposition and grief to a minimum. Jeremy has been great to me, as a boss and a lover, and it's the least I can do to spare him the agony of having to watch me die.

I'm glad he's coming over. I don't have all the words in order just yet, but I take comfort in the fact that I won't have to agonize over it for much longer. He'll come, we'll talk, and then we'll go our separate ways.

DAY 257

All I can say is that life is a cruel manipulator leading us down a road to enlightenment, if we are lucky. I think about that idea often, a little over six months now since the last time I saw Jeremy.

He never made it to my house that night when I received his excited phone call. I had expected him in thirty minutes and thought nothing of his tardiness until three hours later. Since I had met him, he was seldom late. But he was spontaneous and reactive, and sometimes his schedule did not proceed as planned. I figured it was one of those times. At eleven o'clock that evening, I started to worry. I had tried calling him a dozen times and got no answer. I wanted to drive over to his place, but I didn't want to come across as a smothering girlfriend. It didn't matter, as he wasn't there anyway.

I got the call from his sister at just past midnight. I was still awake, still thinking endlessly about my predicament, when I answered the phone, and she told me Jeremy had been in an accident. I asked if he was all right and where he was, and she held back the details from me. I couldn't understand why. She was crying and trying to talk and not making any sense, and I yelled at her through the phone that she should get herself together and just tell me. I wish now that she had held firm and kept the details to herself, locked away for eternity.

The details I did get were more than enough. While driving over to my apartment, a semi truck loaded with oranges hit Jeremy's car head-on. The driver had dozed off and as his head dropped, the steering wheel turned ever so slightly to the left, directing the truck over into the oncoming traffic. Jeremy was likely killed upon impact, his car reduced to a metal cube. As if that wasn't enough, the metal cube burst into flames to ensure that any trace of him was thoroughly destroyed. Maybe that was for the best. There was no need to go to the hospital, no need to see him suffer in a hospital bed, and no need to look into his eyes and see the fear of death. It wasn't much, but it was something.

A week later, there was a private celebration held for him, and his mother made sure to invite me personally. At first, I thought there was no way I could go, and no possible way I could make it through such a sad and emotional situation. I was devastated, heartbroken, and had just completed my first round of radiation. I needed to sleep but couldn't. I was sick, through to my core, and I thought the vomiting would never end, but his mother insisted and I'm glad she did. At the celebration, I learned from his sister and his mother just how close Jeremy and I had become. They each shared with me their individual discussions with him and how he wanted their approval of his commitment to me, and what they said made me cry. What they said also made me realize it was worth it. Against all odds, both of us had made the effort to go with our hearts, with what we felt was right, and to act upon feelings regardless of what anyone else might think. That realization gave me the strength to carry on and fight, so I could live another day.

I completed the rounds of radiation and chemotherapy and, somehow, it appears the treatments have worked. The cancer is gone for now, my hair is returning, and I'm just taking life day by day. When I am alone late at night and I look out upon the stars, I see Jeremy's face and it's the face of that first night when he drove me home and I kissed him on the cheek. His expression was so youthful, innocent, and hopeful. I see that face in my mind, and it always makes me smile. Surprisingly, the ghost face of my husband has left me and when I think of him, I can remember the night of our first date, when he took me home and I kissed him on his cheek. I have the love of these two men to carry me forward and I am hopeful about the future.

At the end of the day, the meaning of love, of life, is merely the sum of all the loves that you have, and have had, and I know now that I am not quite complete in my effort to define that meaning. Maybe I'm just getting started.

NOTES ON
AT THE END OF THE DAY

On January 29, 2012, I awoke at 4:00 a.m., exactly. I was wide awake, a feat quite unusual since I almost always sleep through the night, unscathed and uninterrupted. It was a dream that woke me, but more than that, it was a story. Over the years, on those rare occasions when I have woken in the middle of the night, seldom was I conscious enough to remember or persistent enough to think about what I was dreaming. Usually, I just went back to sleep, and the dream or the thought disappeared forever.

This time was different. This time, as I lay awake in bed, the dream and the thoughts would not escape my mind and only grew in intensity as the minutes passed. After half an hour of trying to get back to sleep, I accepted the fact that my mind was not ready, so I went downstairs to my office and proceeded to write up a two-page story idea.

The next day, I walked into my office and sat down in front of my computer. On the screen, I saw a document that was foreign to me. It was my standard story idea template, but I didn't remember working on one. I read over that story idea and synopsis I wrote, and a funny thing happened: I began to remember. Just seconds earlier, I had no memory at all of what happened after I went to bed the night before. But as I sat there at my desk, I remembered getting up and going into my office to write, though I couldn't remember the words. As I re-read what I wrote, the words and the story came roaring back, and I remembered clearly. You know what else? I thought it was a good story idea.

I get many ideas for stories, and I try my best to write them down. They can come to me at any time and if I don't write them down, they're not real. If I don't write them down, they get lost. Maybe the lost ideas still linger in my subconscious to return at another time. But maybe they won't. I can't take that chance. So, I write them down and I review them periodically, and it is usually very clear which stories I have to write. It's those ideas—the ones that blaze in my mind and don't let me think of anything else—that I *need* to write. Such was the case with the idea for *At the End of the Day*.

It is a mystery to me why this dream, this particular idea, woke me that night. All I can say is that I cannot even control what I think about when I am awake, so my subconscious mind is a true rogue warrior. It is on its own and does what it wants. Whether I am asleep or awake, the ideas pop into my head at will, and I have learned to just go with them. It could be worse. I could be a writer with no ideas at all.

A couple of months later, I juggled my schedule around and got to work on the story. I knew who the two characters in the story were, and I knew what each of them wanted. I felt I just needed to put them together to see how it would play out. I knew I wanted the story to be narrated in the first person, present tense, but I wasn't sure which character should narrate. The man's point of view would be the obvious and easiest choice, but I felt that the woman had something to say, something important.

Jim Harrison is one of my favorite authors, and I remembered reading an interview in *The Paris Review* in which he talked about writing the novel, *Dalva*. Two-thirds of the story is told from the perspective of a part-Sioux woman in her mid-40s. It took Harrison three years of preparation before he was comfortable that he had the appropriate voice of the woman character. I didn't have three years and I wasn't writing a novel, but I wanted to give it a try. So I decided to switch back and forth between the individual perspectives of the man and the woman, exposing what each of them was feeling at different times in their relationship. I wanted to learn about each character's fears, concerns, passions, and perspective on love.

At the End of the Day is a love story. It's a story of forbidden love, and it's likely a story to which we can all relate. Social norms often guide us in our relationship decisions, but in the fictional world of the written story, those norms and expectations are less rigid. I needed to find out what would happen if the two characters pursued a relationship that they, or anyone else, would never think was possible. I'm glad I found out.

I realize there is a writing lesson to be learned here. I need to write down my ideas, and I need to listen to my subconscious. There's good stuff (and a lot of it) in there, and I need to write the ideas down as they come to me, so I can add to the pot of gold in my head. I know that if I didn't write down this particular idea, I likely would have lost it forever, like so many other passing thoughts. Fortunately, I did write it down, and the idea wouldn't leave me alone until I listened and told the story.

OUT OF TOUCH

They stared at each other like young lovers; only their ages were at issue.

They sat in a dark corner of the bar, a sufficient distance from the other patrons to afford them some privacy, yet close enough to get the attention of the bartender if, or when, the need for another drink arose. The drinks had been flowing for most of the night and would likely continue. She didn't need it, but he would likely benefit from the courage that the alcohol would provide. It was late, and the room was mostly quiet. Only a few hushed conversations were in play as the bouncing head behind the piano tickled out a near-silent serenade.

"It's quiet here," he said.

"Yeah, it's nice," she replied.

"So, vodka, huh?"

"Yeah."

"You always drink vodka?"

"What do you mean, 'always'?"

"Nothing," he said. "I just wondered if vodka was your liquor of choice, so-to-speak." *Liquor of choice—where did that come from?*

"I've been drinking it tonight," she said. "You know, it's kind of a special occasion."

"I know," he said. He stared at the label on the beer bottle in his hand as though it might provide some advice. "I wasn't sure I would show."

"Why?"

"I don't know. It's been a long time. The last time I saw everyone was at prom, a lifetime ago."

"Yeah."

"It's the last time I saw you." He took a long draw from his beer. He felt the urge to burp but held it back.

She looked deeply into his eyes and studied his face, expecting the sound, and was surprised when it didn't come. "You remember the last time?"

"Like it was yesterday."

They each looked down at their drinks, not wanting to make eye contact while they took themselves back to a special day a long, long time ago.

He glanced up for just a second, saw her smile, then he looked back down before she could catch his glance.

"So where've you been hiding the last twenty-five years?" she asked.

"Oh, I've been around."

"Always the modest one," she said. "The last I heard, you moved to Paris, but that was a few years ago."

"I'm still there. It's been ten years."

"Do you like it there?"

"I did for a while."

"No more?"

"Not so much."

"Jeff Horvath filled me in," she said. "I ran into him at a party." She thought about what she'd said. "It's been ten years? Hmm." She looked perplexed. "You remember Jeff?"

"I remember," he said with an expression of displeasure.

"What?"

"I saw him tonight, and I regressed into a pimply teenager."

"*Really?*" she said. She wasn't sure what he meant.

"He hasn't changed a bit."

"He's a little gray," she said.

"He actually came up to me and flicked my ear, like he did a thousand times when we were younger." His face turned red, and he shifted in his seat. He took a drink and tried to swallow his anger.

"Are you okay?"

"I walk into the hall, and he's the first person I meet, like he was waiting for me. Before I could say a word, he flicks me. Then I looked around and saw the staring faces and the snickers."

"I'm sure it was nothing," she said.

He looked at her with unyielding eyes.

She thought she saw him inch toward her. "Sorry, I didn't mean to interrupt."

He took another drink, then waved to the bartender with a circling index finger. "I don't know how to explain it. When he flicked me, it was like he tripped a switch inside my head. It just happened."

"What?"

"I punched him in the nose."

"No."

"Yes." He sat up straight in his chair and his regular color came back, along with a dash of bravado.

"That was you? I saw him running to the bathroom with a red handkerchief up to his face, and I just thought he had a nosebleed or something. That was you?"

"Sorry," he said.

"No need to be sorry. It's about time someone stood up to him." She looked straight into his gaze and smiled coyly, excited by the excitement.

"Let's talk about you," he said.

"Oh, there's not much to talk about."

"Now look who's modest. You went off to UCLA to study film-making. Where that came from I'll never know. Three years later, you're in Hollywood and starring in a film."

"I wasn't the star."

"Whatever. You were in a film, in Hollywood. I went and saw it the day it came out."

"You did?"

"Of course. You were my girl. I had to see how you turned out."

"You're so sweet."

"Funny thing is, I tried to keep track of you over the years, but it was like you disappeared."

"Don't be silly."

The bartender arrived at the table and set down a fresh round of drinks.

She cleared her glass quick and handed it to the bartender. "Keep 'em coming," she said in a delicate voice.

The bartender left.

"You have time for another drink, don't you?"

"Sure," he said.

She grabbed her fresh cocktail and swallowed half the contents. "Tell me about Paris."

"What to tell," he said as he pondered her inquiry. "My wife left ten years ago. We got married after college, and we both worked hard at our careers. We had no kids, and there really wasn't anything there, no relationship to speak of. So on the day of our tenth anniversary, her present to me—to us—was my freedom."

"I'm sorry."

"No, it was good. I packed up and left for Paris the following week. I needed a change of pace, of venue. My art needed it. And I've been there ever since, enjoying the life of an expatriate and a wannabe Parisian."

"It seems to suit you."

"It's been fine, great actually, up until about two months ago."

She looked at him curiously.

"Two months ago," he said, "when I received the invitation for the reunion."

Her glassy eyes were empty. The words weren't registering.

"I received the invitation and immediately threw it away. I was in Paris, for Christ's sake, and what could I do? The funny thing was, like a week later, out of the blue, I thought of you." He looked at her for a reaction, but none came. "I called Tina Thompson to inquire about the RSVP list, and that's when I found out you would be attending, alone."

She cleared her glass again, swirled the remaining ice cubes and stared at the glass, disappointed. "Bartender!" she yelled to the table-top.

As if on cue, the bartender arrived at the table and set down a fresh round. She handed the bartender the empty glass.

He studied his accumulating beer bottles. "Thanks," he said to the bartender, who was already walking away. He turned back to her. "So I dug the invitation out of the garbage and reconsidered. The thought of coming back kept me awake for weeks. I couldn't think. I couldn't work. I was done for. What was stuck in my head was that last time we were together at the lake, lying together in that big green sleeping bag and watching the sunrise. I couldn't shake it. Do you remember?"

"Oh, I remember."

"So I called in my RSVP, and here I am."

"Yessiree, here you are."

"I don't think you get it. I came back for you."

In one fluid motion, she cleared her glass once again. She set the glass down and reached across the table to touch one of his hands. "You're so sweet, coming back for little ole *me*," she said through a burp. She blushed. "*Excuse* me."

"I can tell there's something there, between us," he said. "From the moment I first saw you this evening, I knew. When we shook hands and then hugged, I knew. When I felt your body next to mine on the dance floor, your warm breath on my neck, I knew. I felt a stir inside of me that I haven't felt in a long time. I knew."

"Too much time has passed. We *can't* go back," she said.

"Sure we can. Your idea of 'going our separate ways' was wrong. We should have stayed together."

"We can't go back."

"Sure we can."

"NO, WE CAN'T!" she shouted, as errant spit flew across the table and hit him on the cheek.

He pretended not to notice. "But . . ."

"You're so sweet," she said in a calmer voice. "Before you go any further, I need to tell you something."

"What?"

"There's no easy way to say it, so I'll just come out with it. After that night, our last night together, I *had* to leave for California."

"I know. You had summer school."

"No, I *had* to leave . . . because I was . . ."

"What?"

"I was pregnant."

"No."

"Yes. I went to California to have an abortion. I was too young. *We* were too young. I had an abortion and pretended like you and the baby never existed."

"No."

"Yes. I went to school, I met a few influential people in Hollywood, and I slept my way right to the top. I became an actress, a film star, and then just when I thought I'd made it, it all fell apart. I started doing tricks on Sunset Boulevard just to make ends meet. I started doing heroin and cocaine and got caught up in a world you couldn't imagine."

The bartender arrived with another round of drinks. Their table was the only one still occupied to keep him busy.

"Get lost," the man said to the bartender.

"But leave the drinks," she said. She leaned across the table and touched his hand once again. "I'm sorry."

"What are you saying?"

"You sweet thing."

"What?"

"I'm a prostitute."

"No."

"Yes. Half of your old classmates that you saw tonight, they're customers. In fact, I think I've had them all. All except you."

His face turned red again. He emptied one of the bottles in front of him, then grabbed another and guzzled half of that one. "It doesn't matter. I don't care."

"Now you're downright adorable," she said.

"Really, I don't care. That's in the past. You could quit that life. You could come back to Paris with me."

"Oh, I couldn't."

"I'll take you anywhere you want to go. We'll leave all this, everything, behind, and we'll start fresh, the way it was supposed to be. You know I'm right. We were meant to be together."

"But . . ."

"I love you," he said.

"The magic words. You sure do know the way to a girl's heart. Why don't you settle up the check, and then you can take me to your hotel room so we can discuss our future together." She gazed at him as she licked her lips.

The dance floor feelings stirred in him again, and he waved anxiously for the bartender. He instantly felt that waiting any longer could prove problematic, so he jumped up from his chair and pulled a wad of bills from his pocket. Without looking, he peeled off five bills and threw them on the table. "Let's go."

As she started to rise, she caught a glimpse of movement from the bar entryway. She glanced over and then she sat back down.

"What's the matter?"

"We have guests," she said.

"What?" He looked toward the entryway to find two men approaching their table. He wasn't sure what to make of it.

The two men approached in a hurry. One of the men was older and distinguished and was dressed like a businessman. The other man was taller and twice as broad, with shoulders and arms that strained the material of his white, pressed smock.

The distinguished man spoke first. "Darling," he said to the woman.

"Can I help you with something?" the man said in reply. "We're having a private conversation here."

"I'm sure you are," the distinguished man said. He turned to the woman. "Darling, it's late, and it's time for you get back to the home."

"Excuse me, but she's not going anywhere. I've already hit one guy tonight, and I'll—"

"Sir, I commend your chivalry, and I'm sure you feel you're doing the right thing, but this is my wife."

"What?"

"My wife of twenty-two years, and it seems she put the slip on the guards tonight."

"The guards?" the man said.

The distinguished man looked at the woman. "Darling, you've been a bad girl, haven't you?"

She didn't say a word.

The larger man stepped up next to her, folded his tree-trunk arms across his chest, and looked down at her.

The distinguished man continued. "It seems she's been planning this evening for quite some time. When she didn't show up for her medication this evening, the orderlies became suspicious. They searched her room and found the invitation and the checklist she used to secure her escape. It took a little while, but it was fairly easy to track her down here. I apologize for any inconvenience she may have caused."

"Did you say *escape*?" the man said as he looked at the larger man. He noticed an identification badge pinned to the larger man's chest, and he squinted in the dim light to read it. "The MacMillan Institute?"

"Sir, unfortunately, my wife has struggled with mental illness for the better part of our time together. She's been a resident of The MacMillan Institute for the last ten years."

"No."

"Yes. For some reason, she felt compelled to attend her high school reunion. How she received the invitation in the first place, I'll never know. Again, I'm sorry for the inconvenience."

"But . . ."

"Darling, it's time for us to go."

The larger man grabbed the woman under the armpit and lifted her like a feather-filled doll.

She hiccupped just once as she ran a hand across her flat stomach to smooth out the material of her sleek, black dress, then she gently lifted each breast so they were both appropriately positioned. She looked at the man with a sparkle in her eye. "This was fun," she said. "I'll see you later?"

The larger man escorted the woman from the table, and the distinguished man followed.

The man remained standing at the table as the bartender approached. The man looked at the bartender as though in a daze, as if he had been sucker-punched. From across the room he heard a scuffle, and he turned.

The woman was straining under the grip of the larger man. She said, "Billy?"

The man looked at her quizzically.

"Billy?" she said again, this time with an edge of desperation in her voice.

"It's Tom. Tom Fitzgerald," he said.

She stared blankly for a few seconds, waiting for the short circuit to repair itself. "Tom, I'll wait for you," she said, and with that, she and her entourage disappeared from the bar.

"Sir, can I get you anything else?" the bartender said.

"Huh?"

"Can I get you anything else? It's last call."

"Yeah, sure. I'll have what she was having—a double." He slowly sat down as the bartender walked away. It was only then that he noticed he was alone, again, and left wondering what had happened.

NOTES ON
OUT OF TOUCH

Life happens at a breakneck pace, and it's easy to get caught up in whatever is coming next. We are each brought into this world with a pre-defined plan for life—school, career, possibly a family, car, house—and before you know it, you're standing at the end of a road and wondering where the time went. You look back and struggle with the reality and try to put the pieces together of how you got there.

When the challenges of life weigh you down, it's easy to look back on an earlier time, when life was simpler, happier. We've all done it. You may look to the past and think you want to go back to the way life used to be, but more often than not, sensibility kicks in and you realize that the past is best left behind and instead you turn around and forge ahead on down the road.

In *Out of Touch*, a simple invitation to a class reunion is all it took to send the protagonist back in time, like he was waiting for it. Memories of youth and innocence and young love came roaring back and he had no choice but to attend. Maybe it was fate or his destiny, and he felt his desire to reclaim his first love was not quite out of reach.

Life is not always what it appears to be, and I like exploring the more obscure possibilities in my stories. That was certainly the case with *Out of Touch*. I knew it was obvious my main character would be out of touch, simply given the span of time that had passed since his graduation from high school. But I wondered if he could be out of touch beyond the obvious. And what about everyone else? A lot can happen in twenty-five years.

I was inspired to write this story after reading the Hemingway short story, *Hills Like White Elephants*. His is a story of two characters, a man and a woman, and their dialogue-driven encounter while sitting at a table at a train station. In the story, very little is said about what is going on outside or around them, for it's not important. Their names are never revealed, and it doesn't matter. There is a man and a woman, and they are talking about something very important. I especially loved how Hemingway could make a statement without the characters saying much at all. Through effective word choice and an expectation that the reader would make the effort to look into the minds of the characters, Hemingway was able to create a compelling and thought-provoking story, and it's all in the dialogue.

So, I wanted to write a story that was purely driven by character and dialogue. I put a man and a woman at a table in a quiet bar at the end of the evening. They had just attended their high school reunion, and I wanted to find out what would happen. When I first started the story, I knew the history of the man and what he was looking for. She, on the other hand, was a blank slate and without any of my own doing, she very quickly drew in the lines, creating a picture that no one could expect—not even me.

OUT OF TOUCH

I did not go to my high school reunion. I can't say I really wanted to go, and I excused myself because I was caught up in other things, in life. I do think it would be interesting to see all of my past friends and classmates, but then again, it's been a long time. I've been out of touch, and maybe when you're that out of touch, it's best to keep it—and ensure it stays—that way.

LETTING GO

The buzz in the coffee shop had quieted. With the morning rush over, only a few solitary customers remained, nursing old coffee and wasting the morning away.

Sebastian Drake sat alone at a square table by the front windows, staring out. The morning sun, which was harsh and lit most of the room, had driven the other customers away from him and into the darker and deeper rear section of the shop. He wore dark sunglasses and a black suit that had seen better days with a black t-shirt underneath. His hair was clean today, and he wore his outfit with confidence. He swirled the remains in his cup while watching the traffic go by.

A middle-aged man entered the shop and made a beeline for the counter. He gave his order to the young man behind the counter, then shuffled down to wait for his drink. He looked like any of a thousand others who walked the streets of downtown on this morning or any other morning. The uniform he wore was standard issue: dark blue suit, white shirt freshly pressed from the cleaners, red tie, and black leather shoes with a blinding shine. He worked in high finance, or was maybe a lawyer. Regardless, he looked like a successful businessman.

A coffee drink appeared at the counter where the businessman was standing. He grabbed it, turned, and walked to the front of the shop. There were twenty open tables in the front section to choose from, only one occupied. He chose the occupied table.

"Mind if I join you?" the businessman asked. He stood by the chair opposite Drake and waited.

Drake turned from the life being played out in the street and looked up at the man. He scanned the room, then returned his gaze to the stranger standing before him.

"Are you serious?"

"You're Sebastian Drake," the businessman stated, firm and direct.

"And you're interrupting. There are plenty of other tables."

Before another word was spoken, the businessman sat down across from Drake. He gave Drake the once-over, sizing him up, then took a sip of his coffee while continuing to look directly at him. Drake returned the gaze, the corner of his mouth twitching, his jaw clenched.

"You don't recognize me," the businessman said.

"Should I?" Drake's patience was thin.

"St. Peter's Elementary." Drake wasn't impressed, and he ignored the man, who tried again. "C'mon, we went to school together."

There was silence. Then Drake said, "St. Peter's—that was over thirty years ago." Drake remained tense, ready for anything.

The businessman sipped again, then set his coffee down. "I need to talk to you."

"I need you to move along."

The businessman reached inside his suit jacket, removed something from the inside pocket, and slid his hand down while it was still behind the veil of the lapel. He continued gazing directly into Drake's sunglasses and smiled. There was a loud click.

"Sebastian, please, humor me," the businessman said.

Drake slowly raised a hand and reached for his sunglasses. He removed them and set them on the table. "My name is Drake, and why don't you put that toy away before you hurt yourself."

"I wouldn't call it a toy. It's a Walther PPK, .38 caliber. It's small, but it sure is effective. Given where it's aimed, I would think you'd be concerned."

"You think you're James Bond?" Drake said.

The businessman chuckled. "You're funny. You always were. I can assure you, though, if you don't play along, you won't be laughing." The businessman smiled and stared.

Drake stared back, unconcerned, his eyes a radiant shade of blue, yet bloodshot and showing the effects of the previous night's binge.

"You look terrible," the businessman said. "It looks like the bottle is getting the best of you."

"And you look like Ray Parsons," Drake replied.

Ray Parsons grinned wide. "Now that wasn't so hard. I knew you would remember me."

"How could I forget?" Drake let go of his sunglasses and slowly reached under the table.

"What are you doing?" Parsons was startled and immediately uncomfortable.

"I put my finger in the barrel of your gun."

"What, are you crazy?" Parsons was beside himself.

"I saw it in a cartoon once. It caused the gun to backfire into the shooter's face." Drake cracked the hint of a smile.

"You're insane. One twitch of my finger and your late-night sexual escapades are over."

"Like I said, you're Ray Parsons, and I know you don't have it in you. Besides, look around. There are witnesses. You don't go and threaten someone in a public place. Put that thing away and tell me what's on your mind." Drake kept his finger in the barrel of the gun and leaned back in his chair.

Parsons' discomfort became more evident as a heavy film of perspiration rose on his forehead. He wiped his forehead with his free hand and then wiped the hand on his pant leg. His hand was still moist, and he looked at it as though it was leprous. He raised the hand and waved it at the counter across the room.

"Hey, Timmy, be a good kid and get me a glass of water." Parsons turned back to Drake.

It so happened that Timmy's name was actually Jacob. Insulted, Jacob grabbed a glass, added ice and spit, and filled the glass with water. Drake saw everything. Parsons didn't have a clue. Jacob walked over and set the glass of water down on the table in front of Parsons. "There you are, sir." He waited a moment, then disappeared. Parsons raised the glass to his lips.

"Don't drink that," Drake ordered.

Parsons froze. "What?"

"Loogie." Drake gave a slight nod of his head toward the glass.

Parsons lifted the glass and peered from the side. Clinging to a chunk of ice, the green-tinted garnish peered back.

"Timmy," Parsons said through gritted teeth. He turned to find a deserted counter, then he turned back to Drake. "Thirty years ago, you would have let me drink it. Might even have spit in it yourself."

Drake didn't say anything as they remained connected, finger to gun. Uncomfortable seconds passed.

"Take your jacket off and relax," Drake suggested. "It's gotten a little warm in here."

Parsons stared at Drake, then looked down as if he could see through the table to the gun in his hand. He continued to perspire. He looked back up at Drake and remained still. The successful businessman was losing his edge.

"I was sorry to hear about your mother," Drake said.

Parsons thought about it, then nodded. He seemed to relax some. "I saw you at the church. You made a good effort to not be noticed, but not good enough. Why did you show?"

"I read the obituary in the newspaper. She was a good woman."

"You didn't know a thing about her."

"I used to know her. I used to know you." Drake paused as he removed his finger from the barrel of the gun and folded his hands in his lap.

"Are you sure you want to do that?" Parsons asked. "It was your only defense."

"I'm sure. Why are you here, Ray?"

"You used to be so perfect, thinking you could take on the world. And now look at you. Why are *you* here?" Drake detected aggression building in Parsons' voice. Parsons continued, "Bigshot Northwestern graduate, degree in journalism, investigative reporter for the *Chicago Tribune*—back when it was still respectable, a Pulitzer Prize; you were a man on top of the world." Parsons took a sip of coffee, grimacing as it went down. "The coffee here sucks." He swallowed hard a couple more times, as if trying to bury the taste. "Tell me something, Sebastian."

"Call me Drake."

"Tell me something, Drake. Where did you disappear to for those two years after Northwestern and before you started at the Trib? For the life of me, I couldn't find out anything about you during that time. It's very strange."

"I can't remember. It was a long time ago. I think I recall having to go out into the world to *find myself.*"

"Yeah, find yourself. Very funny. Anyway, after the Pulitzer, you decided to go creative and became a novelist. You've written three novels, none of which are very good. I did buy a copy of each of them. You're welcome."

"Thanks," Drake said. "Are you going to start up my fan club?"

"In the last year, your publisher dropped you, and now you live alone in a loft over on the wrong side of town. Not so perfect."

"What's your point?" Drake asked.

Parsons went for his coffee again. As he lifted the cup, Drake bolted up from his chair, grabbed the table at the corners closest to him, and rammed it into Parsons' stomach. Parsons grunted loudly and projected a storm of spit from his lips. Everything on the table flew at him. The tainted water spattered his chest and the glass fell to the floor, bouncing a few times but remaining intact. Drake's sunglasses and empty cup followed. Drake was next to Parsons a second later, connecting his elbow forcibly into Parsons' jaw. Parsons' gun arm was pinned to the back of the chair and his grip loosened, and before he could fully process what had just transpired, Drake laid a hand on the Walther, twisted Parsons' wrist unnaturally, and took control of the gun.

"What—what did you do that for?" Parsons rubbed his jaw with his free hand and shook off the fog in his eyes.

Drake saw the expression and thought of a Led Zeppelin song from his past: *I've been dazed and confused for so long . . .*

Parsons snapped out of it and tried again with a whine. "Hey, take it easy, I was just kidding."

"This gun makes me think you were quite serious." Drake inspected his new acquisition and liked it. Looking down on Ray Parsons, he saw a man defeated. "If you don't mind, I'll just hold on to this." Reaching behind, he stuck the gun in his waistband and pulled his jacket back over it. Parsons pushed the table away and whimpered.

Behind the counter, Jacob reappeared as if from thin air. Towel-drying a coffee mug, he looked over at the front table, smiling.

At the table, Parsons was rubbing his wrist. "Jesus Christ, you could have broken it." Using his suit jacket sleeve, he wiped spittle from his lips and tried to compose himself. "Where the hell did you learn to move like that?"

"Boy Scouts, eighth grade," Drake replied as he walked over to his chair, which had fallen backward to the floor, and bent to pick it up. He reached down again for his sunglasses, but left the other fallen items, and then pushed the table back to its original location and sat down again opposite Parsons. He folded his hands in his lap and stared as though nothing had happened. As far as the other patrons were concerned, nothing *had* happened.

"What, are *you* James Bond?" Parsons asked.

"Now I am. All I needed was the gun," Drake said with a face of stone. "Ray, what's on your mind?"

"You wouldn't understand."

"Let me take a shot at it. You left the old neighborhood after eighth grade. You went to a private high school out east, just outside of Boston. You grew out of your uncoordinated, klutzy phase and made the high school baseball team. By senior year you were an All-American third baseman. You must have hit the books as well, because you were accepted to Harvard, studied law, and were the editor of the *Law Review*. You were recruited by the biggest law firm here in Chicago, and now you're a full partner. You live with your wife and two daughters in a fancy house in Lake Forest. Overall, you've done quite well for yourself."

"How do you know all that?" Parsons asked.

"I read the papers." They looked at each other. "I have to admit, though, I'm stumped as to what we're doing here. Is all your success too much to handle?"

"Don't play ignorant, Drake. You know exactly why I'm here."

"You're going to have to enlighten me."

Parsons looked down at his red tie, now water-soaked to a cranberry hue. He shook his head, disgusted. "Everything I've done over the last thirty years, everything I've become, all the success I've realized, is because of you."

"You're welcome."

"Drake, everything I've done, I've done in *spite* of you."

"Sorry, you lost me again."

"Remember what good friends we were when we were younger?"

"Sure, I remember." Drake wasn't sure where this was going.

"I looked up to you, wanted to be just like you. You were a good friend. You helped me learn how to hit a fast pitch. You got me through that damn 'new math' we were learning at the time. You were popular, and I was a geek, yet you always went out of your way to include me. Then you left." Ray Parsons once again became an insecure teenager.

"Ray, I had to leave. You know that. My father got his transfer orders, and he packed us up and shipped us off to the naval base in San Diego. It wasn't the first time. Three years earlier, it's what brought me here to Chicago, to the old neighborhood."

"You left me there with those animals. Without you around, everything changed. I was a social outcast. My grades suffered. I started getting my ass kicked on a regular basis again. My life became a living hell, all because of you."

"Ray, it was eighth grade. Thirty years ago."

"That may be true, but everything changed after that."

"Seems like you turned out all right."

"Once the schoolyard beatings started, my father joined in. You'd think he'd have been supportive, maybe stand up for me. No, he just called me a sissy and smacked me in the head. He told me to toughen up. It got so bad that my mother left him. We ran, found a new place to live, a new school, a new life. My world was turned upside down. After a couple of years, things started to get better, and I vowed that I would do whatever I had to in order to get back at you, to be more successful than you."

Drake shook his head with a mixture of disbelief and compassion. "That's quite a grudge."

"I can't believe you hit me."

"I can't believe you pulled a gun on me."

"I wasn't going to use it. I just wanted to scare you a little, make sure you listened to me." Parsons rubbed his jaw and worked it back and forth to make sure it was still hinged correctly. He felt his bottom lip and looked at his fingers. There was no blood.

"You could have introduced yourself politely," Drake said.

"And what? You would have hugged me, told me how good it was to see me, and offered me a seat? I don't think so. You're different now."

"I'm not that different, but you're probably right." Drake spun his folded sunglasses on the table in front of him. "Look who's talking. *You're* different."

Parsons cowered a little. "I know. I have some anger management issues."

"You think? You've got to let it go, Ray."

They both sat quietly, contemplating what had happened. Neither of them wanted to speak again. Enough had been said already. Silence engulfed them.

Drake smiled, then laughed. Parsons looked up from his lap, saw the grin on Drake's face, and laughed himself. Their laughter swelled so that everyone left in the coffee shop could hear them, but they didn't care.

Behind the counter, Jacob was drying another coffee mug and shaking his head. "Nut jobs," he said. He put the cup away and went about his business.

Drake and Parsons calmed down and quieted. They sat looking at each other.

"I know it was a bad idea to come here. I thought if I could see you, talk to you, and maybe rub a little of my success in your face, it would make me feel better. I thought it would allow me to move on. My wife told me I needed to confront my past, my demons. Otherwise, the anger would continue to eat away at me. She said I'd never be truly happy."

"How did it work out?"

"I feel worse. Listen, I didn't mean what I said."

"Sure you did."

"No, I know you must be going through a tough time."

"I'm fine, I assure you. I'm living my dream, the life of a struggling novelist."

"Well, I guess I should be going." Parsons adjusted his tie and jacket and rose from his chair. "We should get together for a drink sometime. Who knows, maybe we could be friends again."

Drake showed no reaction at all.

"I know, don't push it," Parsons said as he hiked up his pants, turned, and headed for the exit. He reached the door, stopped, and turned. "Maybe I'll see you around."

Drake grinned. "It's a big city."

Parsons nodded, turned, and walked out of the coffee shop. He paused at the sidewalk to take in a deep breath of the crisp morning air, and he looked up at the cloudless sky as his edge seemed to return. He crossed the front window and disappeared down the street.

Once again with disbelief, Drake shook his head as he reached for his sunglasses. He put them on and returned his attention to the morning unfolding in the street before him.

NOTES ON LETTING GO

Back in the latter part of 2009, I was mulling over ideas for a future writing project. I was rummaging through my files and came across some notes I had jotted down for a crime thriller that I hoped to write some day. I've always been a fan of the mystery genre and crime mysteries in particular, and I thought it might be fun to venture into that genre. Over the years, I have especially enjoyed those books with protagonists who were so interesting and compelling that they could come back again and again in subsequent stories. There are many characters who, over the years, have influenced my reading and writing habits. Raymond Chandler's Phillip Marlowe and Dashiell Hammett's Sam Spade laid the foundation for me. But then there were those characters with their secrets and past lives who were called upon to solve someone's problem. There was Lee Child's Jack Reacher and Randy Wayne White's Doc Ford that did it for me. These were characters who grabbed me and forced me to return to each new novel that was published so I could find out what they were up to and what was coming next.

Secrets . . . we all have secrets, don't we? It was with that thought that I set out to develop a character who I hoped could possess the depth of personality, appeal, past experience, and skills necessary

to solve a crime in a new, exciting, and thought-provoking manner. The character needed to have a robust and juicy skeleton in the
closet, one that needed to stay hidden but that ultimately had to be
exposed. I had some ideas for the character's secret past, but then I
remembered something my daughter had told me regarding a comment one of her friends had made about me after she told him I was
a writer, about him thinking I might be a spy, or something of that
nature. I can't imagine how he got that idea. I am not a spy and never
have been, but wouldn't it be fun to find out what it might be like? *A
writer with a secret government past . . . Hmmm . . . Interesting.*

My character would need a name, and while coming up with an
interesting name is always a challenge, I tend to go with whatever
pops into my head. I felt that in this case, the name needed to be
unique, different, telling, and memorable. I thought for a moment,
the idea popped, and that was it.

In April of 2010, Sebastian Drake was created.

The story, *Letting Go*, was my first effort to find out for myself
who Sebastian Drake really was, and what he had the potential to
become. I needed to know what he was doing now, and at the same
time, I needed to get some insight into his past, his demons, his
special skills, and his possibilities for the future.

I sat down in front of my computer, pictured Drake in my mind,
sat him at a table in a coffee shop, and set the wheels of imagination
into motion. When I finished the story two days later, I found that I
had created more questions than I'd answered. Actually, I'm not sure
I answered many questions about Sebastian Drake at all. But I was

intrigued by what happened in the story and I thought I might want to know more. Actually, I *needed* to know more.

Subsequently, in January of 2012, I wrote a twenty-two-page screen treatment based upon *Letting Go,* which outlined the screenplay I was going to write for a feature length film titled *A Fine Line.* Sebastian Drake was going for the big screen. It took me a year, a lot of long days, and a severe amount of cutting, and the final revision of the screenplay was completed in May 2013.

At each step along the way—the short story, the screen treatment, and the screenplay—the character of Sebastian Drake had become more interesting, more challenged, and I was compelled to find out what was next for him. He simply would not leave me alone.

I've often said that as a writer, I don't always get to write the stories I necessarily want to write. More often than not, I write the stories I *need* to write. Something (or someone?) in my head nags at me until I finally give in and get to work, and ultimately, until the deed is done. Those ideas and characters that repeatedly pop into my mind direct me as to what I will work on next, and Sebastian Drake is on my mind a lot.

I had recently embarked on a project to bring Sebastian Drake to his ultimate story platform: the novel. In a reverse adaption and using the screenplay as a basis (the same process that I used for my first novel, *Recalled to Life*), I am happy to say that as of this writing, the initial draft of *A Fine Line: A Sebastian Drake Novel* is complete. After a few more revisions, and after Sebastian Drake has finally closed this chapter of his story, the book will be published, and we'll

see where it goes from there.
     Who knows where he will take us.

THE DARK SIDE

All he knew for sure was that he felt strange, somehow lost in a way he could not explain. He felt emptiness in his gut unlike any he had ever felt before. It was dark and cold, and while there was no one around, he felt that there were others in the distance. He saw nothing, but after a while he could hear them, whispering. He hugged himself and rubbed his arms, but that did nothing to comfort him.

A stranger spoke. "Robert?"

"What?" There was faint breathing from beside him, and it made him uneasy. "Who's there?" He looked around and saw nothing but infinite darkness. He had never seen darkness so black. It was as if someone had turned off the universe. He thought the voice sounded familiar but could not place it. The voice was gravelly, old. He wondered if he'd heard the voice at all.

The old voice spoke again. "Do you go by Robert or Bob?"

He spun around, searching. There was nothing, and he became very afraid. "Who are you? This isn't funny. Turn on the lights. I mean it!" His fear morphed into instant rage.

"I'm sorry, but there's nothing I can do about the light at the moment. I'm here to help you, though, if you'll let me. Tell me your name."

"Bobby, I go by Bobby," he barked. His defense mechanism was on high alert. He heard a nervous tension in his voice, and that added to his anger.

"Very well, Bobby. It's nice to finally meet you."

"If this is some kind of sick joke, there's going to be hell to pay." There was no response. "I mean it," Bobby added. He thought he sounded tough and mean.

"Bobby, please. Just relax, and I'll help you through this. I'm the only one here who can help you. I'm the only one who *will* help you."

Bobby tried to calm himself. He had been mad before, and he could usually feel the anger, the rage pulsing in his temples. Today, he felt different. It was more fear than anger.

He thought back to when he was a young boy, trying to hide from his father. He usually picked a closet, a different one than the last time. He sat inside and as far back from the door as he could, the hanging clothes resting on his head. If he had time, he cleared the floor first. Otherwise, the shoes and boxes bunched up underneath him. He sat there in complete darkness, his eyes ablaze, pupils expanding. His ears pulsed in unison, reaching out like giant satellite dishes searching the heavens for any sign of life.

Sometimes he had a minute, sometimes ten, to sit alone in the darkness and silence. When he thought about the silent closet time, he realized it was the only time he was truly at peace. However, the serenity he felt always fled the moment he saw the thin bar of light underneath the door. He thought it strange that he always heard the click of the light switch after he saw the light, and it was that click that sent his heart racing. He pushed himself further and further back, wishing he could push through the wall, and he listened.

He knew they would come. They always did.

He heard one footstep, then silence. Then another step and again, silence. Each footstep sounded like it came from a gigantic lead boot, and Bobby envisioned an ancient and giant underwater diver, wearing a large round metal helmet with a hinged faceplate and an oxygen tube that floated up into infinity. Each step he heard sent a thundering vibration through the floorboards that rattled his spine. The skin at the base of his neck tightened and came alive with a warm tingle. The footsteps came closer and closer, and his gaze remained fixed on the light passing under the door.

First one shadow appeared. Another followed and then the footsteps stopped. He thought he heard two similar, yet somehow very distinct heartbeats pounding in his eardrums. The sound was too much to bear, and fear overcame him. He had a way of dealing with his fear, and it was at this point that he simply gave up, shutting off all of his senses. He thought only of the single word, 'NOTHING' (his father had often said he was good-for-*nothing*), and nothingness filled his mind. He relaxed every muscle all at once and just let go. Warmth surrounded him.

"Bobby? Bobby, stay with me," the old voice shouted.

"Huh? What?"

"Are you okay?"

"Yeah, sure." The closet memory would not fade. A miserable

sadness overcame him, and he began to cry, quietly. Oddly, he felt no tears.

"Bobby, it's natural to feel that way. The feeling will never pass, but you'll learn to live with it."

"Who the hell are you?"

"My friends, if you can call them that, address me as Max. I guess you could say it's a nickname—one bestowed upon me a long, long time ago. The others found my surname difficult to pronounce, and I just don't think they liked it."

"Max, I'm only going to say this one last time. Turn on the God-damn lights!"

Max sighed. "Oh my," he said while reaching out for Bobby. He felt him, letting him know that it would be all right.

Bobby felt Max's soft touch and calmed.

"I'm sure you have quite a few questions, Bobby. I'm all yours until it's time for you to be on your way." Max remained close and comforting.

Bobby wanted to think long and hard, but that was not his nature. He spit out the first thing that came to him. "Where am I?"

"The dark side," Max said.

"The dark side?"

"Of the moon, of course," Max added.

"Very funny. Just when I calm down you have to go and piss me off again. What in God's name are you talking about—Max, is it?"

"You're a God-fearing man, are you?"

"Hell, yeah," Bobby said.

"Oh my," Max replied.

Bobby thought about it for a moment. "All right, wise guy, if we're on the dark side of the moon, where are all the stars? You know, all the other stars in the *universe.*" It came out like YOU-niverse. Bobby felt like a genius.

"Bobby, I'm not sure I can explain it to you." Max paused. "The shadow that's cast upon us, by *THE* light, is a shadow that is impenetrable."

"Impenetrable?" Bobby felt stupid.

"No light can come in; no one can see out. That's just the way it is," Max said.

Bobby did not understand but also did not feel like arguing. "All right, I'll play along," he said. He had to be dreaming. It was the only explanation. There was no point getting all riled when he would be waking up any minute. He might as well enjoy it, for shortly he would be up and at it, heading off for another dreadful day at the quarry. "So, Max, I'm on the dark side of the moon, you say?"

"That's correct."

"And how did I happen to get here? I suppose I just flew here on a rocket ship?" Bobby laughed.

"You could say that."

"I could?"

"Bobby, listen. That's not important. What's important is that you're here now, with the rest of us."

"The rest of us?"

"You hear them, don't you?"

Bobby listened. There was a faint hum of a million whispers. The sound irritated him like an itch he could not scratch. "How 'bout we tell them all to shut the hell up."

Max sighed again. "I really wish you wouldn't talk like that."

"I don't care what you wish. If you want to help me, tell them all to shut up or just wake me up from this God-damn nightmare."

"Whoops."

"What?"

"That kind of talk won't do you any good here," Max said.

There was an uneasy pause.

"I'm sorry, Bobby, but I don't have the ability to quiet them. You'll learn soon enough that we have to talk, need to talk. It's the only way to make our time here bearable."

"So, Max, what did I do to deserve this?"

"You have to ask?"

"I'm asking."

Max started to feel that this was not going to be so easy. He had seen all types. Nothing surprised him, but Bobby was off to a slow start. "What is the last thing you remember prior to meeting me here?"

The whispers quieted, and there was silence. Then the hum of whispers returned and grew louder.

"Bobby, did you hear me?"

"I heard you. I was thinking."

"And?"

"And, I can't remember."

"Bobby, let's not make this difficult. Why do *you* believe you're here? Think. What is the last thing you remember, the last time you were angry, really angry?"

"It was *him*," Bobby said.

"Him? Who?"

"You know who." Bobby was getting agitated.

"Your father?"

Bobby did not say anything.

"Bobby, your father died twenty years ago. You're a grown man. Don't you think it's time to let that go?"

Bobby remained quiet. He did not feel so grown up.

"Bobby, I'm only going to say *this* one last time. Why do *you* think you're here?"

"Couldn't say."

"Couldn't say or wouldn't say?" Max pressed him.

"Couldn't say." Bobby was holding firm.

"Bobby, think. The alley, the dumpsters, the darkness, the cold."

"Sorry, nothing."

"The struggle, the rage, the kicking and scratching, the scream—does any of that ring a bell?" Max waited for an answer.

"Oh, that," Bobby said.

"Now we're making progress."

"But it wasn't my fault."

"No?"

"NO!" Bobby yelled so loud he thought his eyeballs would pop out. For a split second, he wondered if he had eyes at all. The emptiness in his gut was replaced with hot, needle-piercing pain, as if he was being stabbed with a flaming sword. He wanted to reach out, grab Max by the throat, and strangle him. He wanted to punish him for making him feel this way again. He reached into the blackness with arms he was not sure were there and groped desperately. He grunted as the animal rage returned. The blackness in his eyes turned to a shade of red so hot it made him scream. "NO! It was because of *HIM*! I mean, it was because of *HER*! SHE MADE ME DO IT!"

The whispers stopped. Darkness and silence engulfed him. After a while, the pain subsided but would not go away completely.

"No, Bobby, it was you," Max said in a voice so calm, almost feminine.

"But—"

"Bobby? The first step is to take responsibility for your actions."

Bobby started to weep. This time he could not control himself, and his sobs rang out around him. The whispers returned in a full orchestration that seemed to soothe him as he wept.

"Max?"

"Yes, Bobby?"

"Can you help me?"

"I can help you . . . to help yourself."

"Tell me what to do, Max. I don't want to be like this, to feel like this any longer. Please, help me."

"Bobby, it's quite simple. The path, while dark, is quite clear. All you have to do is take the first step, then another, and then another. You have but one responsibility here, and that is to walk and to think about what you did. Only by thinking about it might you possibly be able to resolve it, within yourself."

"I'm not sure I understand," Bobby said.

"Walk and think. That's all there is to it."

"What about everyone else?"

"What about them? Everyone here has the same responsibility, the same goal. Listen to them. Maybe you'll learn something. Maybe they will learn something from you." Max could tell Bobby was uncomfortable, but he did not have any more time to spend with him. He had to attend to other business. He gave Bobby a gentle nudge.

"Hey!" The nudge startled Bobby. He curiously thought that the force pushing him was not from a hand, unless it was a hand with only three fingers. The prodding forced him forward a step, but Bobby held his position firm. Somehow, he could tell Max was losing patience.

"Start walking," Max said.

"But I don't want to," Bobby replied. He sounded like an eight-year-old refusing to eat his vegetables. As a young boy, he refused often, which always led to a firm smack upside his head. Bobby twitched. He felt the three-fingered hand on his back again, this time more firmly. He stiffened. The fingers turned to daggers that stabbed him in the back.

"Get moving," Max ordered.

Bobby started to walk. He felt wetness trickling down his back, and he was afraid again.

"That's it. Now you're getting it. Walk and think. Walk and think."

Bobby walked. The whispers turned to voices, and they were all around him. He turned.

"Hey, Max?"

"Yes, Bobby."

"How long do I have to walk, uh, and think?"

"You have to ask?"

"I'm asking."

"Forever, Bobby. Forever."

Notes on
The Dark Side

The short story *The Dark Side* came to me as I was driving back from Delavan Lake on a cold and gloomy day in February of 2010. I had driven up for the day to check on our house there and was coming back in the late afternoon, heading south on I-94 and crossing over from Wisconsin into Illinois. On my way up earlier in the day, I had decided that it was "Pink Floyd Day" for my car ride. The morning music focused more specifically on the solo recordings of David Gilmour, and even more specifically on his *Live in Gdansk* recording. That afternoon, however, I treated myself to *Dark Side of the Moon*, an album I had not listened to in its entirety in quite some time.

Dark Side of the Moon is arguably one of the greatest musical recordings of all time. The stars were in perfect alignment on those special days when the collective talents of four musicians and their entourage magically morphed the sounds of their voices and instruments into analog waveforms that someone ultimately pressed into vinyl for the entire world to hear. Seldom does an album hit the mark on every song as happened on *Dark Side*, and while *Time* and *Money* have certainly become part of our world musical culture, the other tracks are no less remarkable. I listened and understood the magic and the significance of the songs as I drove home that afternoon.

The music of Pink Floyd is intelligent and thought-provoking. It is the kind of music that leaves a lasting impression, where a song can make you recall personal memories of past times and places tied to when you last heard the song. To appropriately archive my musical experience on that particular afternoon, I felt there would be no better way than by writing a story to commemorate the day. My mind instantly veered toward the album title and while driving, I began to think about that cold and dark place. It is a place within the grasp of man, yet for most people like me, it is a distant world set in the background of life, and set mostly in the deep recesses of the mind. The *dark side of the moon*: always out of sight, and always out of reach. The distance, the darkness, the coldness, and the mystery of it all led me to only one conclusion, only one explanation.

A week later, during the first week in March, I set out to explore for myself this dark mystery. I put myself in that most unexpected of places, and I was quickly introduced to Max and Bobby. It didn't take long for Bobby to expose to me his sordid and destructive past, and while I felt somewhat sorry for him, I felt that the penance he was to pursue was apt. Through it all, while Max helped me to understand, I realized that the darkness and the mystery will likely remain, forever, and maybe that is the best possible outcome for all of us.

FOR A FEW LAUGHS

There was a knock at the door. A moment later, the door opened softly. A young, beautiful face appeared in the thin gap.

"Excuse me, Mr. President. Secretary of State McMasters is here to see you."

The President sat stiffly in his chair, surprised. He had served his two terms, but he still enjoyed being referred to by the formal title and appreciated the attention. There was a newspaper in front of him that he really could not read—because of his poor eyesight and lack of interest—and a stacked mess on the corner of his desk. All he could come up with was, "Really?" He thought for a moment. "All right, send him in. And Angie, could you bring some refreshments for us?"

"Of course, Mr. President." The young face disappeared and the door closed. A few seconds later, there was another knock on the door.

"Come in."

The door opened and in walked McMasters. "Mr. President."

The President did not get up. He simply barked, "McMasters, you old son of a gun, what brings you to these parts?"

McMasters didn't expect that. "Um, Mr. President, I'm here on a matter of national importance."

The President woke a bit, only slightly interested. "National importance, you say." He looked at McMasters with skepticism.

McMasters did not say anything. He was uncomfortable having to bother the President. The sweat on his brow glistened like a neon sign.

"Come on over and sit down. Relax a little. You look like you're going to soil yourself." The President chuckled a little.

"Mr. President, I know you're busy," McMasters said.

"Busy?"

"I've been monitoring all of your philanthropic efforts. You're quite a busy man," McMasters said.

The President sat up a bit straighter. He was thinking this could be fun. "You're monitoring *me*? Don't you have anything better to do than to keep your nose stuck in my backside?" The President kept a face of stone.

"Excuse me?"

"McMasters, you don't have a clue!" Again, he was a stone, unwavering.

"Mr. President, I just meant to say—"

"I know what you meant," the President said. He paused, and McMasters relaxed only slightly. "I was just having a little fun with you." The President smiled and then got serious. "I've been retired, out of the office, out of the spotlight for, what—almost twenty years now? Sure, I'm busy, but I'm always ready and willing to serve my country. What's on your mind and what can this ex-President do for you?"

"Mr. President, I'm sure you're fully aware of the situation in Iran. Our negotiations with their government have stalled. This morning, they said the hostages will not be released, and there will be no further discussions. In fact, it appears we've been completely shut down, six months of effort wasted."

There was a knock at the door.

"Come in," the President said.

Angie glided in carrying a silver tray of refreshments. She set the tray down on the desk, turned, and walked toward the door. Two sets of eyes darted around, locking on target. Angie exited the room, closing the door behind her.

They both turned to look at each other.

"Please, help yourself," the President said.

"Thank you," replied McMasters, as he remained in his seat, unflinching.

The President sat quietly behind his desk. His elbows rested on the desktop, hands folded and held up in front of his mouth. His single brow created a "v" across his forehead. "What is President Richards' position?"

McMasters stood straight and poised but pursed his lips, conveying a look combining confidence and support with an air of disappointment. It was quite a trick. "President Richards is maintaining his party-line position. He wants us to continue our efforts to communicate with the Iranian government and work toward his goal of long-term peace in the region. At the same time, he is recommending increased sanctions on trade within the area, hoping to cut them off a little more from the rest of the world."

The President asked, "And your position?"

"My position is that I want to get those hostages out of there. I want them all back here on American soil. I'm tired of playing these games with American lives at stake!" McMasters stood as he finished saying this. The President could feel the sincerity, the conviction, and the anger.

"Please, sit," the President said. "So, how can I help?"

McMasters sat and adjusted the lapels of his suit jacket. "We would like you to make a trip to Iran, to meet with the Supreme Leader."

"Really? Why in God's name would you want me to do that? I was the least successful of any President in maintaining stable foreign relations in that area." The President looked at McMasters with disbelief.

"The Supreme Leader asked for you specifically, Mr. President. He said he would only have future discussions with you. I don't even know why the hell I'm in this position. He certainly won't talk to me."

The President sat back in his chair. He laid his folded hands on his belly. His knuckles whitened. His heartbeat quickened, his hands rising and falling with his heaving girth.

"All right, what the hell is this? Did somebody put you up to this?"

"Sir?"

"Don't screw with me, McMasters. The whole world knows of the mutual hatred and discontent the Iranian leaders and I have for each other. Remember the last time I *met* the Supreme Leader at the United Nations conference?" He made quotation marks in the air with two fingers from each hand as he said the word *met*. "That meeting almost started World War III. There's a reason why we haven't spoken since and why our relations with that country have always been strained." Above the v-brow, a vein bulged in the President's forehead.

"Mr. President, I understand the past. I can't say I understand the current request, but the Supreme Leader has assured us that if you will agree to meet with him, he will guarantee the release of our people—within twenty-four hours of your meeting."

The President scratched his head. "Really?"

"Sir, I asked the former First Lady to pack a bag. It is waiting in the car outside. Air Force Two is waiting in the hangar and can leave immediately upon your arrival."

"So you're serious?"

"As a heart attack," McMasters said.

"Don't talk like that," the President fired back.

The President leaned forward, stuck his hand into a mess of papers, and pressed down on something.

"Yes, Mr. President," came Angie's voice from the mess.

The President cleared away the papers, revealing a sleek console with enough buttons to control a space launch. "Angie, cancel all of my appointments for the next forty-eight hours. I'm going to Iran."

"Yes, sir," Angie replied.

"And please pull the files from my past trips."

"Yes, sir." Launch control went silent.

The President put his hands down on the desk in front of him and pushed himself up from his chair. A few bones cracked as he straightened, but the movement would do him good.

The President asked, "Will you be going along for the ride?"

"I wouldn't miss it for the world. Plus, I think it's my job." McMasters stood up, a bit more relaxed now, grinning.

"This could be good for a few laughs," the President said.

"Like going to the dentist." McMasters seemed to be impressed with his own quick and witty reply.

"Cut it out," the President said, shaking his head. "A comedian you are not." He walked around the desk and led the way out of the office. McMasters followed quietly.

The most painful part of the trip was the limousine ride over to the base. Traffic was brutal and the stop-and-go jerking was enough to make the President want to turn around and go home. His neck ached.

Once on Air Force Two, the day calmed. There was a crew and entourage of more than fifty people on the plane, but they left the President and McMasters alone in a private dining room. They had a fine dinner, good wine, and conversation was sparse. The President preferred the conversation that way. The flight was unremarkable as the plane clicked off the miles.

Later in the evening, in one of the meeting rooms, a staff member briefed the President on the ceremony of the next day and the particulars of the schedule. McMasters tried to talk about the latest diplomacy and political intelligence, but the President was not interested. The files that Angie had packed tightly into his briefcase remained there.

The President excused himself and retired to his cabin to sleep. Lying there in bed, he could only wonder why the Supreme Leader had requested him. An answer did not come, would not come, so he thought instead about how nice it was to be out of his office. Back when he was President, he loved getting on Air Force One at a moment's notice and flying off to wherever he was needed or wherever he wanted to go. He reminisced briefly then trailed off to sleep.

The following morning he arose to an annoying alarm. He showered, dressed, and ate breakfast alone. The First Lady was a world away, so he had two fried eggs over easy, crisp bacon, toast with real butter, tomato juice (he only drank the stuff on airplanes for some reason), and coffee with cream *and* sugar. As he ate, he thought about how he would greet the Supreme Leader. What the heck would they talk about? Again, nothing came. He wondered if in fact they would release the hostages as promised. *There has to be a catch. We hate each other.*

Upon landing and after the usual de-planing preparations, the door to Air Force Two swung open. Several staffers, along with Secretary McMasters, exited the plane first. The President stepped to the doorway, lowered his head, and walked through. He stood for a moment at the top of the movable stairway, which descended down to the tarmac. He looked out and was amazed at what he saw.

Thirty yards out, a contingent of soldiers, dressed in full uniform and unarmed, stood perfectly in four identical rows that stretched endlessly in both directions. In front of the soldiers there was a color guard presenting both the Iranian and American flags. Closer still was an impressive military marching band playing a song that was unfamiliar to him, but moving nonetheless. He never knew such a band existed. Closest to him, at the bottom and to the left of the stairs, was an arsenal of photographers from all over the world. To the right were three beautifully dressed and well-mannered children, each holding gifts. The children were similar in features, with short dark hair, olive complexions, and very proper manners. The President figured them to be around ten years old.

The President descended the stairs, holding firm and steady to the railing. *"Having a fall"* down the steps in front of all these people would not make for a good first impression after all these years, the President thought. He made it to the bottom of the stairs without incident and stopped there. He looked around with confidence, smiling.

The children stepped forward. The first child, a girl, handed him a bouquet of flowers. She stepped back as a boy stepped forward, lifting a small wooden box and handing it to the President. As the President took the box, the boy leaned forward and lifted the box's lid, revealing a row of neatly stacked cigars, his *favorite* cigars. The smell of the finely aged tobacco engulfed the President, and he breathed deeply. The boy closed the lid and stepped back. Another girl stepped forward, presenting another box, this one covered with an exquisite red velvet-silk material. The President handed the flowers and cigars to an aide and accepted the red box from the young girl. As the boy had, the girl reached forward and lifted the lid. Inside was a Baccarat crystal bottle of twenty-five-year-old scotch whisky, again his favorite. Feeling like it was his birthday, he beamed, thanked the young children, and waved to all and to no one in particular.

The President heard a car approaching from off in the distance but could not determine its location. Without notice, the crowd on the tarmac parted, each group moving aside in unison. The President saw an ominous and dark limousine of a vintage variety appear from the rear of the crowd, and it sped quickly toward him. Of everyone there on the tarmac, he seemed to be the only one worried about what was transpiring. He felt like he was in a dream, except the car was not moving in slow motion. He questioned what he was doing there, in a foreign and hostile country run, as he felt, by an arguably insane dictator. Everyone in his view was smiling, but he tasted bacon and egg in the back of his throat as the car sped toward him. He wanted to move but could not. He thought about high-tailing it back up those steps and into the plane but did not. *Why isn't anyone else worried?*

The car continued its direct path toward the President. At a distance of twenty yards, the car began to decelerate as it initiated a graduated turn away from him. Before he could think further or make any type of move, the limousine had pulled up in front of him and come to a stop. The President removed the perfectly folded square of fabric from the left breast pocket of his jacket (his wife had told him to never use it, that it was just for decoration) and wiped the perspiration from his forehead. *I hate this place; it's too damn hot*, he thought. It had to be the weather that was overheating him, right? The car continued to idle, yet there was no movement from inside the vehicle. The President stared at the right rear passenger window, tinted black, and he guessed it was at least two inches thick. The glass was not transparent at all, and he saw his reflection, the sunlight bouncing off the perspiration on his forehead. He thought he looked like a lighthouse beacon and quickly dabbed at the sweat. He also noticed, for the first time, that McMasters was standing to his right, just behind him.

The President turned slightly toward McMasters, not losing sight of the limousine. "Where the hell have you been?"

"I've been right here the whole time." There was a pause. "It was very nice the way the young children welcomed you, wouldn't you say?" McMasters made one step forward and was right beside the President.

"Yeah, very nice," the President replied, distracted. Out of the side of his mouth he said, "What's the deal on this car? It looks like it should be making a cemetery delivery. And why all the drama? I mean, it's hot enough out here to dry the piss of a camel. Is anyone going to come out?" The tarmac was silent with anticipation.

Just then, the rear window glided down, revealing an ancient, smiling, and bearded face. The President recognized the man, but for the life of him, he could not come up with a name. McMasters

leaned in and whispered into the President's ear. The President nodded. The door flung open wide, and the ancient man's relic of a hand
waved to both men, motioning them to come. As the President and
McMasters walked toward the car, the old man slid over, making
room for them to enter. They both stepped into the car quickly and
the door seemed to close itself behind them.

The President and McMasters sat next to each other on a bench
seat of finely upholstered leather. The President shifted a bit, enjoying the feeling of the soft cushioning beneath him. Riding backward, they faced the old man, who sat smiling and nodding. Mc-
Masters introduced the President and the old man, both of whom
were leaning forward and being cordial. The President learned that
the old man was the personal assistant to the Supreme Leader. He
had learned this fact the night before on the plane but decided not
to remember it at that time. They spoke few words and settled back
in their seats.

The President leaned ever so slightly toward McMasters, and he
again attempted to talk out of the side of his mouth. "Did you happen to bring that scotch with you?"

McMasters raised a fist to his mouth as though he were covering a cough. "Sorry, Mr. President. That's going to have to wait," he
whispered. "It's on the plane waiting for you on the return flight. I'll
be happy to bartend."

The President straightened and looked across at the old man,
who smiled and nodded. The President thought the old man looked
like a bobble-head doll and wondered if the nodding would ever

stop.

After about twenty minutes, by the President's mental clock, he asked, "Where are we going? The government offices are only fifteen minutes from the airport."

McMasters shrugged. He asked the same question directly to the old man, who, of course, nodded and smiled.

"I could probably tell you if I could see out these damn windows," the President said.

"There must have been a change of location. I'm sure we're fine."

The President looked at McMasters with disappointment and shook his head slightly. McMasters sat quietly with his hands folded in his lap. The old man nodded.

Thirty minutes later, the car came to a halt, and the side door immediately opened from the outside. The old man quickly exited the car and the President and McMasters followed. The President stood at the side of the car for a moment, gazing at the Supreme Leader's personal residence, and he immediately recognized the location. They were in Qom, a holy city approximately eighty miles south of Tehran.

"Just as I remember it," the President said. He turned to McMasters and asked, "When were you here last?"

"I've *never* been here. Since you left office, all subsequent meetings with the Supreme Leader, and all government leaders for that matter, have been held at the government offices in Tehran."

"Well then, this is a special treat for you," the President said.

They followed the old man up a long walkway, into an elaborate garden, and through to a stone archway marking the entrance to the residence. The old man led the way, walking up a few steps and opening a large and rustic wooden door. The old man had to put a shoulder into it, as if he was moving stone. Once inside, the old man waved them in. The President stepped into a grand foyer and McMasters followed. The old man nodded, turned, and continued down a long marble hallway. They walked down the hall in single file, the President three steps behind the old man, who was picking up the pace, and McMasters five steps behind the President.

"Try to keep up, McMasters," the President said, not looking back.

McMasters initiated a power walk to catch up. The President heard the footsteps, turned abruptly, and gave McMasters a stern look that said *there's no running!* McMasters slowed.

The hall seemed endless, but the President was enjoying the walk. The walls were lined with exquisite pieces of art, and the President did his best to take them all in while not slowing. As they reached the end of the hall, they came upon another large wooden door, a double door approximately eight feet wide at its base, coming together at the top to a point some twelve feet above the floor. The President, distracted by the view, caught himself just before he walked right into the old man. He stopped to admire the door. *Exquisite*, the President thought. *Looks like solid walnut. It had to cost a fortune.*

McMasters must have been sightseeing as well and was not quite as quick on his feet. He stepped right onto the heel of the President's right shoe. McMasters jerked back and stood behind the President, much too close and looking blindly at the back of his head. Surprisingly to all (even the old man had to hear it), the sound of the shoes coming together echoed through the hall. The old man stood motionless, facing the door.

"I am very sorry, Mr. President," McMasters whispered.

The President did not turn around. He let out a sigh of exasperation, subtle but effective. McMasters seemed to slouch a bit. The old man remained motionless. After a few seconds of silence (the President thought it more like a minute), the old man raised a bony hand and rapped on the door with a well-practiced three-knock sequence. Silence. The old man waited, while the President counted in his head, *one-one-thousand, two-one-thousand.* At *five-one-thousand,* the old man reached for the doorknob and swung open the right half of the massive door. The President smiled and thought, *always five seconds.* The door swung open without a sound and the old man stepped into the room. The President and McMasters followed. Ten feet in, the old man stepped aside to the left and motioned with his white-robed arm for the gentlemen to proceed ahead. The President acknowledged the old man with a slight bow of his head. The old man responded in kind.

The room they walked into was palatial. The floor and walls appeared carved from a single piece of marble, of an off-white color with gray veining. The ceiling was twenty-five feet from the floor and covered with a mosaic-tile mural depicting an ancient religious scene. Ahead of them were three simple wooden chairs, the seats covered in a refined and cultured fabric. Two of the chairs sat next to each other on the left. To the right, the third chair sat at an angle facing the other two. Next to the rightmost chair was a small wooden table, upon it a simple silver tray that held a crystal decanter and three matching glasses. Standing in front of the rightmost chair was the Supreme Leader, the Ayatollah Sandumar Komeini.

The Supreme Leader looked the part. He complied with the required uniform: a light and flowing white robe and a white turban. He also had the requisite white-gray beard, which made its way down to the middle of his chest. He wore silver, wire-rim glasses at the end of his nose, with welcoming eyes looking over them. He raised his arms from his sides as though he were addressing a large congregation. A breeze from somewhere filled his outstretched robe-wings, animating the flow of the garment.

"Welcome," the Supreme Leader said. He lowered his arms slowly like a drawbridge.

The President walked up to the Supreme Leader and stopped two feet from him. He waited to feel if McMasters was behind him. Nothing. The President extended his right hand to the Supreme Leader and firmly grasped his palm. They shook hands and smiled cordially.

In a quiet voice, the Supreme Leader said, "Mr. President, thank you for coming."

"My pleasure," the President lied. He still was not sure what he was doing there, yet he played along. He stepped aside.

"And Mr. Secretary, thank you for arranging this visit."

McMasters stepped forward and shook hands with the Supreme

Leader. "My pleasure," he said. He lied as well. Although the Supreme Leader had reduced McMasters to an order taker, the President could tell it did not bother him too much. If they could achieve the objective, he knew McMasters would do whatever was necessary to take credit for the success.

"Please, sit," the Supreme Leader said.

He motioned the President to sit. The President stepped forward, stood still momentarily, then they sat in unison. McMasters took the open chair next to the President. The old man was still standing inside the room, close to the door, forgotten. He turned quietly and left, closing the door with a hush behind him.

"Will your President be joining us?" the President inquired.

"Not today. He was adamant about being included in this meeting, but I insisted that we hold it alone. If you have no objection, I would like no other participants."

"I have no objection." The President thought it was highly unusual, but the whole situation was highly unusual.

"May I offer you a drink?"

"That would be nice," the President said. McMasters said nothing.

The table next to the Supreme Leader was on wheels, and he reached over and rolled the table in front of him. "I took the liberty of acquiring a bottle of your favorite scotch—actually two bottles." He grabbed the crystal decanter. "This is identical to the bottle that was given to you earlier. I thought it best not to make you wait until you were back on your plane to sample it. May I pour?"

"Please," the President replied, not questioning whether it was appropriate for the Supreme Leader to be drinking alcohol. Who was he to pass judgment? He turned to look at McMasters. *And you wanted to make me wait,* his eyes said. McMasters shrugged ever so slightly, sitting upright with his hands folded in his lap.

The scotch was poured and distributed. The President held his glass firmly in front of him. Even from a foot away, the vapors rose up to him. He smiled on the inside.

The Supreme Leader raised his glass. "To good health."

The President and McMasters raised their glasses, held them raised momentarily, and then they all drank. The warm liquid burned smoothly down their throats. Each one of them savored the small sip.

The Supreme Leader produced a faint smile. "That's very good. I have never had such a drink, and I am pleased that at this late stage of my life I have had the opportunity to experience it." He set his glass on the table. The President and McMasters held their glasses in their laps with both hands. Neither of them said a word. Silence engulfed the room like a heavy blanket. The President took another drink, as did McMasters. The Supreme Leader folded his hands in his lap and thought for a moment, his head lowered.

Then the Supreme Leader looked up. Gazing at the President, he said, "We do not like each other much, do we." It was a statement, not a question.

"Not much," the President replied. There was no point in holding back.

The Supreme Leader reached and grabbed his glass with two hands, careful not to lose his grip. He took a long drink, savored the taste in his mouth as if he was sampling a newly uncorked bottle of wine, then swallowed.

The President thought, *that's going to hurt.* He took a long drink as well. In his peripheral vision, he saw McMasters drink from his glass. The President straightened in his chair. In the years since he had left office, his confidence had never wavered. His power remained, undeterred. It was time for business.

"We appreciate the opportunity to meet with you today. I expect we will be able to come to some agreement allowing for the release of the hostages." He looked squarely at the Supreme Leader, who did not flinch. Instead, he smiled.

"I would like to make just one request," the Supreme Leader said.

"Of course," the President replied.

The Supreme Leader drank again and then set his glass down. He folded his hands, placed them in his lap, and took a deep breath, the sound of which echoed through the room. Through his demeanor, it was obvious the Supreme Leader wanted to talk.

"Our last meeting did not go well." He paused. "It was a long time ago, but that evening is still fresh in my mind. Do you remember?"

"I remember," the President said. "With all due respect, I hope it will not be necessary to replay how that night ended."

Calmly, the Supreme Leader raised his right hand, attempting to stop the President. "Mr. President, I do not intend to recall how that night ended. That is, as they say, 'water under the bridge'."

"Well, then, what *would* you like to talk about today?"

The Supreme Leader's hand was still raised, fully open and facing the President. He kept his index finger up while curling closed the remaining fingers and thumb. "I would like to talk with you about just one thing." He paused.

"Very well, then," the President said.

"Do you recall how the evening *started?* Fate brought us together at that dinner reception, along with Secretary Miller, the Canadian Prime Minister, and your friend, the Prime Minister of Great Britain. It was an interesting seating arrangement, yet I was honored that I was able to join you." He reached for the decanter, refilled his glass, and with the decanter in hand, motioned to the President. "May I offer you a little more?"

The President pursed his lips and thought for a moment. *What the hell.* He leaned forward, holding his glass out. "Thank you." The Supreme Leader filled the glass, and the President sat back. Both the President and the Supreme Leader looked at McMasters.

"I'm fine, but thank you," McMasters said.

The President made a face, then turned to the Supreme Leader, raised his glass, and took a gulp. He swallowed firmly, let his breath escape slowly through his nostrils, and maintained an unflinching expression. *Take that!*

The Supreme Leader took a similar gulp. The President could see that it hurt him, likely burning his throat like liquid nails, but he respected the Supreme Leader for maintaining a stolid appearance. The President watched as the Supreme Leader held onto his glass with two hands and gave his internal systems time to reset.

Not bad, the President thought.

"Mr. President," the Supreme Leader began. He cleared his throat of whisky-phlegm. "While sitting at your table, I overheard the discussion you were having with the Prime Minister of Great Britain. He is a funny man, always smiling and laughing. You are friends?"

"Yes, I would say we are," the President said.

The Supreme Leader continued. "He seemed to think you were quite funny that evening. I was curious about the nature of the laughter, so I—and I must apologize for doing so—happened to eavesdrop on your conversation as I ate my salad. You were leaning in close, which made it difficult for me to hear, but I have very sensitive ears. Kind of like that superhero you Americans like so much. What is his name, Superman?"

The President was wondering where the Supreme Leader was going with this. His hands gestured to coincide with raised eyebrows, inquiring. His expression said, *okay, and?*

"You told the Prime Minister a funny story, a joke. Do you remember?"

The President thought for a second and quickly replied, "No."

"You told him a joke about a talking dog sitting in a pub. A talking dog . . . very funny." The Supreme Leader started to chuckle.

The President looked at him. He turned to McMasters, who

shrugged.

"Mr. President, you must excuse me," the Supreme Leader said, smiling. "I listened to the whole joke and found it very amusing. I wanted to laugh right then and there, but, of course, that would not have been appropriate. Mr. President, can I tell you a secret?"

The President wondered if he was going crazy. It could not be possible that he was in a meeting with the Supreme Leader of Iran discussing a joke that he could not possibly remember, and that he'd told so many years ago.

"Sure."

"I had to summon every ounce of control to keep from laughing that night. It was terribly difficult, yet I persevered, even though I would have preferred enjoying a simple laugh."

The President asked, "You laugh?"

"I do. Not in public. Laughing does not coincide with the image I am required to maintain. Do you have any idea how difficult it is to repress laughter?"

"I can imagine."

McMasters ran a hand through his hair, frustrated. "Excuse me. I'm really sorry to interrupt, but do you think it would be possible to talk about the hostages?"

The President reached over, patted McMasters on the knee, and said, "In a minute." He half-stood, took a few steps, and reached over for the bottle of scotch with his free hand. He offered to pour for the Supreme Leader, who raised a hand signaling that he had enough. He walked back to McMasters and added two inches to his glass. To his own glass, he added three. "Please, continue," he said to the Supreme Leader, as he replaced the bottle and returned to his seat. He took another swallow from his glass.

"I have not since heard a joke so funny," the Supreme Leader said. "I was hoping you could tell the joke to me today."

The President shook his head in disbelief, but in a lighthearted manner, smiling. "At this time, I think I must concur with Secretary McMasters. We flew here to meet with you to discuss the release of the American hostages." He looked at the Supreme Leader seriously. The alcohol had loosened him up, yet he instantly jumped back into commander-in-chief mode. "I'll have to insist."

"Mr. President," the Supreme Leader said as he chuckled again. "That business has already been addressed. I gave orders to have the hostages packed up and ready, prior to your arrival. My staff escorted them to a room on the other side of the compound and they are awaiting the completion of our meeting. I am hoping we do not have to change our plans."

"All right, let's cut to the chase," the President said, now annoyed. "What exactly do you want?"

The Supreme Leader took a sip from his glass and then held it in his lap. His eyes met those of McMasters. The Supreme Leader smiled a devilish smile like a child knowingly getting into trouble.

"I believe we're done here, Mr. President," McMasters said as he rose from his chair.

Still sitting and maintaining his fixed gaze on the Supreme Leader, the President reached over toward McMasters. After a couple of mid-air misses, he grabbed hold of McMasters by the elbow. "Just a minute."

The President and the Supreme Leader stared at each other.

"So what you're telling me is—" the President began.

The Supreme Leader raised a hand. "All I ask is that you kindly and personally share with me that joke. It should not take long. We will have an innocent laugh together and then you can be on your way . . . with your additional American passengers."

Unbelievable, the President thought. He continued to stare at the Supreme Leader, trying to determine if he was serious. He turned to McMasters and said, "Have a seat."

McMasters sat, begrudgingly. As he ran his free hand through his hair again, he looked down at his glass. He shook his head faintly and took a drink. He whistled as the scotch vapors came back up, then he cleared his glass.

The President took a long drink, cleared his throat, and began. "There was a dog seated at the bar of a local pub, and he asked the bartender . . ." His memory was good, and the words flowed like he was a master storyteller.

The Supreme Leader's assistant was standing guard outside the room when he heard an unusual sound coming through the door. He thought he heard laughter but knew that was not possible. He pressed his ear to the door, listened intently, and confirmed his suspicion. His aged hand bolted from his side and reached for the doorknob. Without delay, he turned the knob, put his shoulder into the door, and pushed it open with all his might. The door swung open and the old man flew into the room. He staggered momentarily as he attempted to stop his forward motion. He looked at the three men sitting at the other end of the room. The President was standing bent over with a hand on his knee, holding himself up as he laughed—a deep and hearty laugh that came from his belly. The Supreme Leader, who was still seated and reclined, let his head fall back as he laughed uncontrollably. Even McMasters was laughing, although he was trying to suppress it.

McMasters lifted his glass and took a drink, hoping that would help him to maintain some composure. As he did, the Supreme Leader wailed with a rat-tat-tat-tat laugh signifying pure hilarity. Unfortunately, the sound of the Supreme Leader's unusual laugh happened to make McMasters laugh, and he choked on the scotch still in his throat. He caught it in time, tightening up like Fort Knox to prevent an outpouring of his drink. However, he could not contain it all, as he noticed a drip of scotch coming out of his left nostril. The President and the Supreme Leader took notice of McMasters's plight. They settled for a moment, made sure he was all right, and broke out again in a full roar. The scotch-out-the-nose made the situation even funnier. The old man stood inside the room, frozen, his mind unable to suggest an appropriate response. After a moment, he hurried forward toward the Supreme Leader.

"It's all right, everything is fine," the Supreme Leader said to the old man. The Supreme Leader felt caught in the act. He tried to calm himself and attempted to maintain a more regular breathing pattern. It was difficult. "I have not laughed like that in a long time, since I was a young boy." He calmed himself and sat, straightening his robe and his turban. As his breathing settled, he reached up and nudged his glasses up to the bridge of his nose. He stood again.

"Our business is done here." To the President and McMasters he said, "I hope we can put our past differences behind us." To the old man he said, "Please see these gentlemen out and join them with our other American guests. Be sure they get to their plane without incident and see them off." He walked over to the President and McMasters. "Thank you for taking the time to visit me today." He bowed slightly.

McMasters stepped forward quickly. "It was our pleasure," he said. He shook hands with the Supreme Leader and stepped back.

"Thank you for your invitation and your hospitality," the President said, and he motioned with his head toward the bottle resting on the table. He smiled.

"You are very welcome," the Supreme Leader said as he reached for the President's hand. He grasped it, shook it warmly, and smiled.

The old man turned and led the way out of the room. McMasters followed, and the President brought up the rear. When he reached the doorway, he turned around and looked at the Supreme Leader.

The Supreme Leader said, "Give my sincere regards to President Richards."

The President nodded. The Supreme Leader nodded. The President turned, walked out of the room, and continued down the hall.

As Air Force Two took off, a celebration ensued. They served food and many drinks as the hostages reunited with their brethren.

The crew and staff were amazed and could exhibit nothing but the highest respect and praise for the two men responsible for the hostages' release. There was hugging and kissing and storytelling. Many of the stories started with fear and terror, but they all ended with smiles and happiness. After a couple of hours, the hostages retired to their individual sleeping areas where they settled in for the remainder of the flight.

The President and McMasters remained, standing alone at a large round table littered with a celebratory mess. On top of the table was the red velvet-silk box given to him by one of the young Iranian girls. It was open, and the crystal decanter was on the table next to it. There was more air than liquid in the decanter.

"I think I'm going to call it a day," the President said. He set his glass down on the table.

"Quite a day it was," McMasters replied.

"Did you have any idea, of the Supreme Leader's request?"

"No. I thought he would make some unreasonable demands, you would promise—on behalf of President Richards—what you did not have the authority to promise, and we would all walk out with the hostages. Actually, although you didn't know it, President Richards had extended full authority to both you and me to ensure we could secure the hostages."

"Nice. Thanks for telling me."

"Mr. President, let me just say that it was an honor and a privilege to serve with you on this mission." McMasters choked up a little bit.

"McMasters, the pleasure was all mine. You're a funny guy. I actually enjoyed spending the last day with you."

McMasters set his glass on the table and they shook hands. The President walked away toward his stateroom.

"Mr. President?"

The President turned around. "Yeah?"

"Maybe I could call you again some time to get involved in another small project of ours?"

The President thought about the question as he put his hands in his pockets. He looked at McMasters with a smile.

"Anything for a few laughs."

NOTES ON
FOR A FEW LAUGHS

I was inspired to write the short story *For A Few Laughs* by a sparsely publicized political event that occurred in August of 2009. Hearing the news of the event instantly planted the seed of a story in my head. The impetus to go ahead and write the story came to me as I sat in front of the La Grange City Hall building, having a coffee on a quiet summer afternoon and taking a break from my morning writing session.

I recalled sitting at the kitchen table a day earlier, having my morning coffee and reading the newspaper before heading to the office. The television station interrupted the morning news with a breaking story. President Bill Clinton had flown to North Korea in an effort to release two journalists and U.S. citizens who the North Korean government had held hostage for many months. His plane had just landed back on American soil and the hostages were de-boarding the plane. It was a touching event and yet, for some reason, I had the feeling it was a politically orchestrated media event.

As I watched, many questions came to me. Why did they ask President Clinton to go, after being out of office for eight years? Was President Obama busy with other matters and was there no one else from his administration available to make the trip? Hillary Clinton was the current Secretary of State and seemed a more appropriate dignitary. Did she have other plans at the time, and did she ask President Clinton to go in her place? The news story that played out over the twenty or so minutes that I watched was a great story, but it seemed too simple, too perfect, and maybe just a bit too orchestrated. Maybe I was just being skeptical.

The next morning, there was full coverage of the event in the newspapers, yet little detail of the excursion that led up to it. A day earlier, President Clinton hopped on a plane, met briefly with North Korean leader Kim Jong Il, and came home with the prisoners. It was as simple as that, a piece of cake. But why were there no details of the meeting? In the paper, there was also a picture of President Clinton and Kim Jong Il. While they both appeared quite serious, the fact that they had their picture taken together at all made me wonder. Of course it was a politically motivated photo-op for the North Korean government, and maybe for the U.S. as well, but both leaders seemed comfortable being part of the event.

So that led me to think about the possibility that there were other motivations, known only to a select few, and the premise for the story *For A Few Laughs* was born. I am sure there was nothing more to the actual event, but I thought that *if there was something more*, it could make for an interesting short story, and it could be fun. I ran back to the office and started typing.

Like most stories I have written, I started thinking that I could finish *For A Few Laughs* in one sitting. However, also like most stories, it took much longer. As I wrote, the characters and the storyline grew and the story took on a life of its own. In this case, some twenty-five or so pages later, written over a few days, the story finally concluded. I like the result. The story is serious and humorous, explores some interesting characters, and (spoiler alert! – stop here if you have not read the story yet!) it has a surprise ending. Who doesn't like a surprise ending?

I did have one concern in writing the story, namely that I felt it might appear I was being disrespectful to the Office of the President of the United States of America, for which I have nothing but the highest respect. While the character of the President is purely fictional, I wanted to do my best to ensure that I retained respect for the position and the office. I hope that in the end I was able to accomplish that objective while still sharing a thought-provoking and enjoyable story.

Adiós Amigo

They raced through the sweltering and congested streets of downtown Guadalajara on their way to catch a flight they would surely miss. They were at the mercy of their young taxi driver who navigated through the rush hour traffic with expert care. At four o'clock in the afternoon, the streets were gridlocked. Their driver seemed to be making some progress, swerving here, cutting back there, and riding the shoulder in some places to gain a few meters. There appeared to be a million cars on the road that day, half of them original Volkswagen Beetles. That model had been out of production for some time, yet it roamed the streets of Guadalajara like it was the latest and most fashionable car one could have. The distinctive toy-like rumble of its engine could be heard throughout the town.

Al Cohen and his wife, Margie, sat in the back seat of the taxi and held their breath, partly because of their young driver's aggressive driving habits and partly because they were jammed in there like two stuffed sausages. The four-door subcompact comfortably sat three adults in the back, as long as they were of childlike stature and weight. Riding comfort would not come this day for Al and Margie. Together, they filled the back seat at its width, and their stomachs pressed firmly against the seats in front of them. Al was breathing heavily, and the young driver moved ever so gently with the rocking sea of Al's belly.

The summer sun warmed the pavement and the street air. The heat mixed with the exhaust as it rushed into the open back windows. The car had no air conditioning, and like an oven, hot and dry air circulated within its confines. Al and Margie both perspired heavily, and their clothes changed colors as unpleasant odors emanated from them.

While quite uncomfortable, they were both somewhat relieved to be on their way home. The week had come to an end, though it did not come soon enough. Al had worked more than he had vacationed, and Margie spent most of her time alone at the pool, making sure her fair skin was covered and hiding under an umbrella. They were out of their element, in a world of language and culture to which they could not adapt. They motioned through each day in agony, waiting for the next and longing to go home.

"I sure am glad to be out of that cockroach-infested hotel," Al said to Margie. "The next time Frank wants someone to work the expo in Mexico, he can send the young kid."

Margie listened but did not respond as she gazed out her window.

"I'll be damned if I'm going to bust my hump trying to sell to a bunch of people who can't even understand what I'm talking about."

He turned to Margie. "Are you listening to me?" he said as he gave her a slight nudge.

"There weren't any cockroaches," Margie said, uninterested.

"What do you mean? Remember that first night when I thought I saw one in the bathroom?"

She didn't reply and instead returned her gaze to the people, the sounds, and the cars.

"Are you listening to me?" Al asked her again, raising his voice.

"Yes Al, you're right," she replied.

"I'm right? Right about what?"

Again, there was no reply.

"Oh great, now you're ignoring me?"

"Al, I just don't want to talk about it. It's been a long week, and I just want to get home."

Al's boss, Frank, had let him know three weeks ago that he would be working the show in Mexico this summer. Frank made it sound like a great opportunity, and he would even spring for the extra plane ticket so Margie could go along. He made it sound as if Al had earned a special opportunity when, in all actuality, Frank had no other choice. His five other salesmen were working more high-priority accounts and projects. He could either send Al or send no one at all. The decision was a difficult one.

For Al and Margie, the trip was challenging from the start. Neither of them could speak Spanish, yet more often than not, it was the primary language spoken. Once outside of the hotel, they were really on their own, and they were lost. The half dozen or so Spanish words that Al thought he knew only made him sound ignorant, and Margie was too shy to even consider making the effort to communicate with the locals. So she took Al's lead, and most often that approach proved to be unproductive. Their original plans to take in many of the city's cultural sights were scrapped early on, so instead they explored the limited offerings of their hotel.

During the day, Al was at the expo by seven, making sure his booth was ready for the day's visitors. For the following ten hours, Al mostly stood and greeted people as they approached his booth and was ready at all times to pass out a business card and take orders. The booth and presentation materials his company provided him were quite impressive, and they kept a heavy stream of businesspeople coming to him throughout the day. Unfortunately, the man in front of the booth didn't meet the same quality standards. Al's suit was much too small for his growing frame, his shirt was not the right shade of white, and his hair was greasy and disheveled.

If that wasn't enough, Al's greeting did a great job of keeping the people moving along. Amazingly, he didn't notice, but his "Hey, amigo" greeting was not well received. The Mexican businessmen looked at him with bewilderment and kept on walking. Al did make sure everyone received one of his cards, but that was the extent of his success.

Frank had expected Al to get at least a thousand orders over the five days of the expo. Al had been able to deliver that at other shows in the States, but this past week he could only scrape up a hundred and eighty, and those did not come easily. He would have to deal with his performance issue when he met with Frank on Monday.

For Margie, she would wake up late in the morning to an empty bed. She would shower, have her coffee, and get dressed for the day.

After picking one of the three very large one-piece swimsuits she'd bought for the trip, she would put it on and look at herself in the mirror. None of them fit quite right, and none of them looked as good as she thought they did at the department store. She covered her suit with a pool wrap that displayed a colorful tropical bird and palm tree scene, but even with the wrap too much of her white-pink flesh was exposed. After leaving the room, her day consisted of regular trips to the breakfast buffet, lunch buffet, and snack buffet. There were intermingled visits to the pool, where she would sit under a large sun hat and a larger umbrella and work on her crossword puzzles. In her week of vacation, her accomplishments included adding at least another fifteen pounds to her already overloaded frame, reading almost three books, completing a total of sixty-four crossword puzzles, and getting absolutely no tan. She wasn't totally unhappy with her week of vacation, as she had expected she would probably add twenty pounds.

When Al returned from his day at the expo, they would dress for dinner and take their pick of the three restaurants at the hotel. One of the restaurants served only traditional Mexican food and did not have the crisp ground beef tacos that Al liked, so that was not an option. After that the choices were International or Italian. Five straight nights they opted for Italian before they grew adventurous enough to try the International menu. After a rushed, quiet dinner, they would walk the hotel grounds before heading up to the room to watch one of the three channels of programs that they could understand. Al was usually snoring by nine, and Margie stayed up late to read one of the romance novels she had brought with her.

As they sat in the taxi and recollected the last week of activities, it seemed to both of them that they had been there a month. They were both glad to be going home, back to their routine existence in an environment they knew and were comfortable with. Once they were on the plane, they would be home in five short hours.

After an hour, the congestion eased, and the taxi was moving at a good pace down the interstate to the airport. Al leaned over and noticed that they were going over eighty kilometers, but he still couldn't figure out quite how fast that really was. The landmarks were zipping by, though, and Al was getting comfortable again about the possibility of making their flight.

"Hey, amigo, can you pull over at one of those chicken stands?"

"Señor?" the driver replied.

"Pollo, pollo!" Al shouted at the back of the man's head in his best Spanish accent, exaggerating the enunciation of each syllable.

"Oh Al, we don't have time for that," Margie said. "We'll miss our flight."

"Don't worry, we have plenty of time. We're just going to pull over, and I'll be in and out in a couple of minutes. I'm hungry, and I want one of those chickens."

Al was referring to the chickens that were prepared and displayed at many roadside establishments in and around the Guadalajara area. They were usually not very elaborate and focused on one thing: roasting chickens. Most proprietors took great pride in their preparations to provide one of the delicacies of the regional cuisine.

"Amigo, right there," Al said as he slapped the driver on the shoulder and pointed to a blinking sign just up the way. He continued to hit the man on his upper arm and point. The man stiffened.

The taxi driver pulled over to the side of the road and brought the car to a halt. Al and Margie lunged forward, Al breathing dangerously close to the driver's ear. Their sudden stop rustled the dust from the roadside gravel. It swirled up, around the car, and into the back windows.

"Hey, amigo," Al shouted to the driver as he covered his face with his hand. Margie was coughing and trying to wave away the dust with both hands.

"Uno minuto, amigo," Al said as he reached for the door handle.

Above the dashboard was a small placard that displayed the young man's taxi license. At the top left corner was a colorful three-by-three picture with an interesting likeness of him, and at the top was his name: Manuel Alejandro Gomez.

Manuel could not understand why this man kept calling him "Amigo". As his passenger tried to squeeze himself out of the back seat, he shared his feelings in his native tongue.

"Huh?" Al said. He wasn't sure if the driver was talking to him, so he tried to stick his head back into the car to hear him. "What?"

Manuel knew his passenger would not be able to understand him, so he went ahead and told him how he really felt.

"What's he talking about?" Al said to Margie.

"He's applauding you for your fine sense of their regional cuisine."

"Whatever," Al said as he stepped back and slammed the door.

"You'll have to excuse my husband," Margie said to the driver as she leaned forward a bit.

Manuel looked at her in his rearview mirror and saw the expression on her face, and he thought he understood what she was feeling.

Al shuffled up to the storefront's open window counter as Manuel and Margie watched. They could see Al trying to communicate to the proprietor, and the volume of Al's voice increased with each attempt. His arms were in full motion as he tried to use them to convey words he could not say. There were at least a dozen chickens turning in a golden-lit and glass-walled rotisserie display, and they moved up, back, and around in a slow rotation while each individual row of chickens turned on its own spit.

Al had his eye on one chicken in particular, currently the second row up, on the far left. He pointed and shouted, like a small child begging his mother for something at the grocery store. "Right there, I want that one," he shouted.

The proprietor was a middle-aged woman with dark hair, a dark complexion, and a round head. She cleared the counter and said nothing. She simply shook her head.

"C'mon, that's the one I want," he said again, pointing. "Cuánto?"

Again, the woman shook her head.

Back in the car, Manuel noticed Margie shaking her head and looking down at her lap. She looked up again as she heard Al start to yell.

"I—WANT—THAT—ONE," Al shouted with deliberate gaps as though he were speaking to a person who was hard of hearing. "COMPRENDE?"

The woman said something in Spanish, saw the quizzical look on her customer's face and instead tried, "NO READY," in a mimicking, deliberate tone.

"What do you mean, it's not ready? It looks ready. It looks delicious. Just give me that one," and he pointed again and again.

The woman shook her head, continued with a stream of Spanish, and Al assumed the woman was just talking to herself. She grabbed a foil tray from behind the counter, along with a pair of kitchen tongs, and she waited for the particular row of chickens to rotate back to her side. She pointed with the tongs and looked to Al for confirmation.

"Sí, sí," he said. "Now we're talking."

The woman grabbed the chicken, placed it in the tray, and set it on the counter. From behind the counter she pulled out a roll of plastic wrap.

"No, no, that's not necessary," he said as he put his hands over the chicken to stop her. "I'm going to eat that right now."

Not wanting to say anything further, the woman pointed to a sign beside her to convey the price. Al saw it, mumbled something to himself, pulled the money clip from his pocket, and paid the woman.

"Keep the change," he said as he grabbed a handful of napkins and his chicken and hurried back to the car.

The woman mumbled something to herself as she put the money into a till behind the counter. She grabbed a two-peso coin from the till and flipped it into a jar with other coins and bills. Her mumbling continued for a few seconds more.

Al squeezed into the back seat, wiggled some as he nudged up to Margie, and reached back to close the door. He was breathing heavily and rocking Manuel again. He sat for a moment to assess his purchase. The chicken rested nicely on his built-in TV tray stomach and a smile formed on his flushed and perspiring face. Margie looked at him, knew she could not stop what she thought was about to happen, and turned and looked out her window. Manuel was looking at his passenger in the rearview mirror, and he thought he saw saliva dripping from the corner of Al's mouth.

"Let's move. On to the airport," Al directed the driver. Manuel returned to the road and continued on.

Al moved in for the kill, gesturing wildly as he ripped at his prize. He took a wing, put the whole thing into his mouth, and sucked. Seconds later he pulled out the bones, clean as though picked by a band of vultures. He grabbed a drumstick, looked at it closely, and turned to Margie. His arm swung toward her.

"Hey Margie, here, try this," he said as he motioned to her.

She looked at him and saw the drumstick. It was sweating and dripping, and the grease and skin inched its way up Al's hand. Because of all the mess, it was hard to tell where his hand ended and the drumstick began. It looked as though Al had grown another freak appendage.

"That's disgusting," Margie said.

"Suit yourself," Al replied. He said this with a note of cheer as he brought the drumstick up to his mouth.

Margie looked around and down the side of her stomach and noticed that Al had dripped on her. The circle of grease grew slowly on the thigh of her tan stretch pants. She pulled a handkerchief from her purse, licked it, and began to dab at the stain. She shook her head.

Fortunately for Margie, they did not have much farther to go. She saw the sign welcoming them to the airport and felt a sense of relief. She returned the handkerchief to her purse, zipped it up, and rested it on her stomach-lap. She was ready.

Manuel pulled the car up to the curb and quickly got out. He was into the trunk before Al and Margie could even open their doors and had their bags on the curb waiting for them. Al opened his door and struggled to get out, still holding his chicken—or what was left of it—in both hands. As he stood up, he turned back around and set the foil tray on the warm and moist seat, made one final, sweeping wipe with his last remaining napkin, and threw that on the seat as well. He reached for his money clip, peeled off a few bills, and extended them to Manuel, who was returning from the curb.

"Here you go, amigo, and keep the change," Al said as he handed Manuel the money. The meter displayed five hundred and twenty pesos, and Al had handed him five hundred and fifty. The current exchange rate netted Manuel a tip of about three dollars. Manuel got back into the car and waited for his passengers to close their doors.

"Idiot," he said in his best, broken English as he put the car into gear and sped off. The remnants of the chicken stayed along for the ride.

Al and Margie grabbed hold of their bags, walked through the automatic sliding door, and proceeded to their check-in counter. They were relieved to find an English-speaking representative as they approached the long line, and they explained their situation. They had cut it close, and the representative moved them to the front of the line so they could hopefully still make their flight. As they moved forward they could overhear rumblings and comments from the other customers.

The airline representative reviewed their passports, checked their bags, and produced their boarding passes. She said their plane would be boarding in eight minutes and was leaving out of Gate 5. She provided them brief directions and told them to hurry, as the gate was at the far end of the terminal. Al and Margie had to make this flight, for the next one did not leave until the following morning. They shouldered their carry-on bags and hustled away.

As they headed for the gate, they tried to move as fast as their bodies would let them. Running was not something either of them had done in quite some time, but they were able to get up to a fast walk. Their weight jiggled ferociously, and their heart rates quickened. Adrenaline coursed through their bodies and helped keep them at a good pace. After just a minute, they were sweating heavily, and their legs ached. Al had a good five-foot lead on Margie, his determination and focus all but blocking out Margie from his thoughts.

"Al, wait for me," Margie whimpered.

Al kept moving, hearing nothing.

"Al, please!" Margie pleaded. There was a hint of desperation in her voice, and she was on the brink of tears. She slowed her pace to a regular stride and tried to catch her breath. She reached into her purse for her grease-stained handkerchief and wiped her dripping brow.

Al kept moving and was fifty feet in front of her, waddling and bouncing his carry-on bag wildly against his backside. He came to a wall of monitors displaying the latest arrival and departure information, and he strained to find his flight. Just as he was about to pass the monitors, he spotted it. The line reporting the status of his flight was blinking. He stopped to look, his eyes scanning the line from left to right, and at the far right he saw "DELAYED" blinking in a different color.

Delayed? Al wondered how that could be. They had left the check-in counter just a few minutes ago, and everything was fine. He wiped his forehead with the back of his hand, which he then wiped on his pants. It was probably a good thing he'd stopped to look at the monitor, for his heart was working overtime at an unsafe level. He turned to look back down the hallway and saw Margie just now catching up to him.

"What's the matter with you?" Margie said to Al.

He could tell she was angry. "What?"

"I was yelling at you to slow down and wait for me."

"Our flight's delayed," he said, not interested in listening to her.

"Would it be too much to ask for you to just walk *with* me?"

"I said our flight's delayed," he replied in between gasping breaths.

They both stood there, trying to collect themselves. Each was upset for different reasons, and they stifled their urges to lash out. Instead, they remained in the middle of the hallway, in front of the monitors, sweat dripping down and off of them onto the floor. They were motionless, save for the rising and falling of their flabby stomachs as they strained to take in the oxygen their lungs so desperately needed. Their lungs burned, and the air made loud gasping sounds as it entered them and whooshing sounds as it escaped. After several minutes, their heart rates returned to what was normal for them. Al dragged the full length of his left arm across his forehead then circled his hand around to wipe his mouth. Margie dabbed at her face.

"Well, that's just great," Al said. "After all that hurrying and running, it was all for nothing. I'm dirty and sweaty, and now I have to sit in this airport for another two hours."

"Let's just go to the gate and see if we can find a seat," Margie said in a dejected tone. She lowered her head and watched the floor as she continued to the gate.

This time, Al let her walk ahead as he stayed behind and tried to tuck his shirt into the front of his pants. His shirttail was out in the back, and it would have to stay that way. He adjusted the bag on his shoulder and started off to catch up with Margie.

As they entered the gate area, the hallway opened up into a large three-story atrium. The room was made of walls on three sides and was lined with numerous duty-free shops and other typical airport retail outlets. The wall to their left was an open wall of glass, a checkerboard of large glass panels, twelve across and ten high. Through the full two hundred-foot panorama view, you could see a dozen planes and a runway off in the distance. The glass wall angled in as it rose to the ceiling a hundred feet up, which provided a glimpse of the clear blue sky. The afternoon sun shone through the top row of glass and fully illuminated the gate area. Though the glass was designed to prevent heat transfer into the room, on this particular day it seemed to be doing the opposite. The sun's rays had elevated the temperature in the gate area more than twenty degrees, and the cooling system struggled to overcome it.

"Good Lord," Al said as he crossed the imaginary threshold and entered the gate area. "It must be a hundred degrees in here."

"Al, see if you can find us a couple of seats."

As he scanned the room, it did not look promising. It was full of passengers, all sitting. Without haste, he walked to the far side of the gate area, closer to the particular gate their plane was to leave from, and looked more closely. Margie followed close behind.

Near the windows he spotted two available seats, and he bolted for them. They were thirty feet away from him. As he started for them, he spied other movement from the corner of his eye. He continued moving forward, his eyes darting back and forth from the two seats to a spot off in the distance. He strained to focus and saw an older man, loaded with bags and being trailed by his wife and children.

No, you don't, Al said to himself as he picked up his pace.

Al and the old man rushed for the seats like two players in a dodge ball game, the whistle just blown, and each of them sprinting to center court to be first to the ball. The first one there would most certainly knock the other one out. The race was on.

It was short and close, and the old man had a meter lead. He easily reached the seats first and claimed victory by setting a bag on one of them. For Al, the race was not yet over, and while the old man was pulling up his pants, he reached the seats and quickly occupied the one that was open. He squeezed in, his size too much for it, and as he slid down to make contact with the seat bottom, his weight spilled over onto a woman to his right, and over the armrest on his left. In the same motion, he swung his left arm down and casually tossed the old man's bag onto the floor. The bag on Al's left shoulder slid off and occupied the second seat. He pretended the old man was not there and motioned for Margie to come and join him.

The old man stood there, his wife and children at his side. The children examined Al with bewildered eyes, as if wondering where he came from. The old man barked at Al with a string of Spanish expletives. His wife tugged on his arm and hushed him, not wanting to make a scene.

"Sorry, amigo. Finders, keepers," was all Al could come up with.

The old man finished his rant, adjusted himself, and herded his family away from the intruder.

"Al, what's the matter with you? Are you out of your mind? Let that family have these seats." Margie was in front of him, looking down at him with disgust, scolding him with her piercing eyes.

"Have a seat," was Al's reply. He removed his bag, rested it between his legs, and patted the open seat as an instruction for Margie to sit.

"I'm going to use the bathroom," Margie said. She took her carry-on bag with her and hurried off, not wanting to be seen with Al after the commotion he had just created.

Al sat and tried to calm himself from his latest workout. He'd had more exercise in this one day than in the last six months, and his body did not like it. Al stored liquids like a camel, yet on this day his reserve was getting low. Earlier the sweat stains were evident around his armpits and the middle of his back. Now his entire shirt took on a darker color and was moist throughout. Sweat dripped down the backs of his legs and soaked his socks. The odor that surrounded him was foul and pungent, putting the woman to his right in a difficult predicament: leave and give up her seat, or endure the unpleasant man next to her. The woman looked at Al, stood up, and walked away.

That was fine with Al. He thought getting the woman's body heat away from him would make him more comfortable. However, he could not control the sun that was beating down on him through the windows. The sunlight radiated into the room, and it tortured him. He would later regret not putting on sunblock that day.

"What kind of place is this? It's like an oven in here." Al spoke loud enough for everyone around him to hear. Most ignored him.

For the next ninety minutes, Al sat, alone in his own moist and scented cocoon. The air and odor floated closely around him like the dustbowl that surrounded Charlie Brown's friend, Pigpen. He dozed off periodically while trying to read a magazine. Sleep, reading, or doing anything was difficult with the sun and heat on him. He had no other choice, though, as there was nothing that would get him up from his seat, except for the boarding call.

As he sat there, his skin changed in color and form. The ultraviolet rays were turning his pale, exposed flesh to a bright pinkish-red, and all moisture was drawn from his pores. His skin tightened and stretched. A small blister began to form on his forehead at the base of his receding hairline. Perspiration continued to flow from him until his personal well ran dry.

Al's head bobbed continuously, his rubberneck keeping his head moving smoothly from the back of his seat, then down as his chin reached his chest. He was in a deep sleep, dreaming of something he would not later remember. He awoke abruptly to an announcement over the loudspeaker. At that same moment his neck gave way, his chin hitting his chest violently. His head snapped up, and he looked around, still in a daze and wondering where he was.

In time, Al was back with the rest of the world. He looked around then glanced at his watch. The first announcement was in Spanish and was followed by a similar message in English. His plane was boarding. The seat beside him was still unoccupied. *Where the hell is she?* Al wondered if Margie had returned from the bathroom and was now off doing some last-minute shopping. He scanned the room to the extent he could turn his head. He could not see her.

He grabbed his bag and tried to get up. His legs were rubbery, and he used the armrests to push himself out of the chair's clutches. He stood and waited a moment for his legs to take hold. The vacated seat was hot and wet. He reached behind to pull the shirt away from his back and the seat of his pants from his crack. Then he slung his bag over his shoulder, turned, and headed for the gate.

He stopped at the gate counter, reached into his bag, and found their boarding passes. He had Margie's, so he knew she had not boarded yet. He waited by the counter, looking around as two passengers walked in front of him and boarded the plane.

"Sir, can I help you?" came a voice from behind him.

Al turned to see a young woman behind the counter, looking at him with her eyebrows raised.

"Uh, I'm waiting for my wife. She'll be right back."

"Sir, we're just about finished boarding. We'll be closing up the ramp in a couple of minutes."

"She'll be right back. Just wait a minute." Al was getting agitated. *Where the hell is she?* He looked around frantically. His heart began to race. Perspiration would normally have come now, but he was bone dry. He licked his lips nervously, yet there was no moisture. A white froth gathered at each corner of his mouth.

Just then, a man approached. He was dressed in a navy business suit with a crisp white shirt and a conservative, dark red tie. His dark hair was neatly combed, and his brown complexion looked young and fresh. He extended his hand.

"Sir, I'm with airport services. Is there something I can assist you with?"

Al cautiously lifted his hand to the man's and shook.

"I'm just waiting for my wife to get back. She ran off to pick up a few things before we boarded." Al had not seen Margie for an hour and a half, and he had no idea where she might be.

If the man detected anything in Al's demeanor, he did not let on. He returned a slight smile and looked straight at him. "Sir, as you know, the flight has already been delayed and we don't want to delay it any further. If you'll give me your wife's name, I will go find her."

"Her name is Margie. Cohen. C-O-H-E-N. She's about this high," he said as he raised his hand to show the man her height. "She's about my size and has beautiful, brown, curly hair."

The man smiled and nodded in acknowledgement. "Thank you, sir. I will go look for her and bring her to the gate. In the meantime, please go ahead and board the plane. Your wife will be joining you shortly."

"I'll just wait here until she comes back," Al replied, not comfortable getting on without her.

"Sir, I'll have to insist." The man's smile was replaced with a curled lip, his eyes narrowing.

"And I'll have to resist," Al said, happy with his quick reply and liking that it rhymed.

"Sir, please. Trust me. Let this young lady escort you to your seat, and I'll be close behind with your wife. We will not leave without her. I promise."

Al suddenly felt a little bit foolish. "All right. But if you're not back in five minutes, I'm coming back out."

"Fair enough," the man replied.

The young woman came out from behind the counter, took the two boarding passes from Al, and led him by the arm through the gate door. They walked down the ramp, the young woman pulling Al along. They boarded the plane, the young woman now walking ahead of Al. She stopped eight rows in and turned around.

"Here you are, Mr. Cohen, seat 8E." She motioned with her hand and pointed.

Al slid in and sidestepped down the short row to the seat by the window. He set his bag on the middle seat beside him and sat down. He couldn't quite make contact with the seat bottom, so he stood up, raised the armrest, and settled back down.

The young woman hurried up the aisle and out the door of the plane.

Al looked out the window to his right and saw only the tarmac. The gates were on the other side of the plane, and though he tried to look across the aisle and out the other window, he could see nothing. He stretched his neck to see who was in front of him and was surprised to see that the seven rows in front of him were empty. He strained to turn around and look behind him, and he saw four other passengers. The plane was silent and motionless.

He reached up to turn on the air, twisting the nozzle to the left and then to the right. Nothing.

That's just great.

He folded his hands and rested them on top of his belly. His watch was staring at him. Three minutes had passed since he left for his seat. Then five minutes passed. Then seven. As though in a trance, Al watched the second hand encircle the watch dial. He would give it three more minutes.

A flight attendant appeared at the front of the plane. She walked down the aisle, looking left and right at each empty row. As she approached row eight, she looked to her left and saw Al. She had a look of indifference on her face.

"Where is everyone?" he asked.

"Because of the delay, some of the passengers made other flight arrangements."

"What other arrangements? No one told me there were other options. I've been sitting in the oven you call the gate area for two hours. How come nobody told me we had other options?" Al was visibly upset, and his heart quickened.

"Sir, we'll be leaving shortly. Please buckle your seat belt." She continued down the aisle, resuming her pre-flight duties.

A minute later she was back up the aisle. She passed Al and continued to the front of the plane.

Al heard the engines start, and before he could think about it, the plane started to move, pulling away from the gate. "Hey, wait just a minute," he yelled to the front of the plane. He tried to get up, but his spent legs would not cooperate. He grabbed the seat back in front of him and tried to pull himself up, but the seat belt held firm.

As if she had appeared out of thin air, the flight attendant was there in front of him. "Sir, please take your seat." She handed him a folded sheet of paper. "The man that was assisting you asked me to give you this."

Al took the paper and settled back into his seat. Without haste, he unfolded it and read the note.

Mr. Cohen,

I found your wife, Margie. She was at the infirmary. Had a slight case of heat exhaustion but is fine now. We want her to get some more fluids before she gets on a plane. We'll have her on the next plane out. Please enjoy your flight.

Sincerely,

Airport Services

Al sat there in a daze. His stomach churned like a washing machine, bile agitated with the remains of his chicken snack. He felt nauseated. The blood rushed from his head. He felt a damp coolness on his forehead, and he thought he was going to be sick. If he'd had any non-essential fluid remaining in his body, he might have had an accident. *I can't leave without her.*

The plane lunged forward. The engines whined as it moved toward the runway. Al looked out the window and followed the plane's course as it turned onto the runway. After a momentary pause, the plane lunged forward again, this time more violently. The engines screamed as the plane shot down the runway toward takeoff. He could feel the plane leave the ground. He threw his head back and closed his eyes, hoping his sickness would pass. He breathed deeply and heavily, struggling for air. He reached again for the air nozzle and twisted in desperation. Rank, stagnant air drifted through the cabin.

"Hey!" Al screamed, on the brink of a breakdown. "Can I get some air turned on here?"

He spoke to no one in particular, and no one responded. A few passengers from behind him echoed his request. Again, no one responded.

He peered ahead, looking for the flight attendant at the front of the plane, but saw no one. There was only a fixed, unmoving scene and silence.

He tried to get up, so he could have a talk with that flight attendant and set things straight once and for all, but he couldn't move. He reached for the clasp to release his seat belt. There was no clasp. Instead, he found a solid block of metal, into which the other end of the belt was inserted. *What the . . .?*

He searched for a button, a lever, or some kind of release mechanism. Nothing. He tugged at the buckle, then pulled on the belt. It rested firmly under his belly, making it difficult to move in any way. The belt would not give. He wrestled with it for a minute more and then gave up, frustrated and angry. *Why was this happening to him?*

There was a crackle over the loudspeaker above him, and a woman spoke. "Good afternoon, ladies and gentlemen, this is your flight attendant. Our flight time today is four hours and ten minutes, and we'll be flying at an altitude of forty-nine thousand feet. Please observe the illuminated seat belt and non-smoking signs and make yourselves comfortable. When we reach our cruising altitude, I'll be coming through the cabin to offer you a variety of preparations for your enjoyment."

The loudspeaker went quiet. Al thought that was odd. *Forty-nine thousand feet? That's got to be a mistake. What's a preparation?*

"Hey! My seat belt is broken. I can't get it open." Again, he was speaking to no one in particular, and no one answered.

He leaned back in his seat, and his head fell back against the headrest. He turned to look out the window and saw only clouds. His breathing was labored, and he wondered if there was any oxygen in the cabin at all. Though he might have been accustomed to it before, he began to notice the foul odor he was taking on, which made him grimace. His stomach rumbled. Feeling ill, he closed his eyes and tried to forget.

He awoke some time later. Time had passed, yet he could not tell at what pace. The thought of looking at his watch never came to him. He noticed the flight attendant moving around the front of the cabin, and he watched her. She was pulling things from drawers in the wall and filling trays. As each tray was prepared, she slid it into a wheeled cart. When she finished, she wheeled the cart down the aisle. She came to Al first.

"Excuse me. What's going on here?" Al said. "There's no air coming through my vent, and my seat belt is broken. Why are we flying so high?"

"Mr. Cohen, everything is just fine. Let me get through the cabin, and I'll have someone look into those things for you. In the meantime, here's your preparation."

She pulled a tray out from the cart and handed it to him.

Flustered, he fumbled with the pull-down tray in the seat back ahead of him. It came down but stopped abruptly when it hit his stomach. He slammed it back up and reached for the drop-down tray next to him, which came down unobstructed, and the flight attendant set his preparation on top of it.

"What's this?" he asked.

"Your beverage consists of a vegetable and citrus blend. The soup is chicken broth and roasted garlic. I also noticed that you have quite a sunburn, so there's a pain relief oil there for you to put on when you're finished."

She continued down the aisle.

"Vegetable and citrus blend? Do you have any whiskey?"

The flight attendant ignored him and went to take care of the remaining passengers.

Al was starving and thirsty, and while what he stared at in front of him was unusual, it would have to do. He took hold of the drink and raised it to his lips. He downed half of it and lowered it back to the tray. It tasted like V-8 and orange juice, and it wasn't half bad. He licked his lips and enjoyed the salty remnants.

He reached for a spoon and tried the soup. He tried to steady the full spoon but spilled it on his shirt as he raised it to his mouth. *This is not going to work*, he thought. He was alone and was not going to worry about what people might think. As he did many times at home with Margie, he grabbed the bowl with both hands and carefully raised it to his lips. He poured the soup slowly over the rim of the bowl and into his mouth. He breathed through his nose as he swallowed. He devoured the soup as though he hadn't eaten for a year and as if it was his last meal. Then he set the bowl down and wiped his mouth with the back of his hand. He burped loudly, a rush of chicken-garlic gas rising up out of him and into his nostrils. He thought his action was fairly disgusting but returned his attention to his beverage. He finished it in two swallows, set the glass back down, and leaned back in his seat.

He felt a little better, but the air was still stale, and it seemed to be getting warmer in the cabin. Maybe it was the soup.

He let the soup digest for a moment, then reached for the sunburn oil. He screwed off the top and squirted some into his left hand. He squeezed too hard, and the oil gushed out, spilled over his hand, and ended up on his pants. Al swore to himself. With his hand still dripping, he set the bottle down and used his free hand to apply the oil, starting with his forehead and continuing with the rest of his face and neck. It seemed the more he put on, the better it felt, so he applied it generously. He lathered his arms in the oil and felt a comfortable tingling. He had not noticed the sunburn at all, but whatever was in the oil made his skin feel good, refreshed, and supple.

He held his arms out in front of him and noticed how they glistened. Before his eyes, the pink flesh turned brown. The sunburn dissipated and was replaced with a light suntan. He looked at the bottle, which had no label, and thought it was quite a product, unlike anything he had ever seen or heard about. He took the bottle and slipped it into his bag. That made him think of Margie, who was always slipping things into her bag. He had not thought about her since the plane took off, which made him feel guilty. He wondered how she was doing and when he was going to see her again. He worried about her, being alone with no one to take care of her, and his stomach began to rumble again.

The loudspeaker came to life.

"Ladies and gentlemen, this is your captain. We're experiencing a mechanical malfunction on our right main engine. We have been unsuccessful at getting the engine back up to full power, and we are going to have to make an emergency landing. Please remain in your seats with your seatbelts fastened. Please give your preparation trays to the flight attendant as she comes down the aisle. I'll provide further instructions and updates periodically."

The loudspeaker went silent again.

There was an outburst from behind him, and Al listened to the other passengers voicing their concern and discontent. He said nothing. He was scared, and he just sat there looking at the back of the seat in front of him. Beads of sweat dripped from his forehead as he felt the cabin temperature continue to rise. His odor returned, and his shirt started to change color again.

He heard the plane decelerate but noticed no movement downward. The deceleration continued for what seemed like several minutes. Then the engines died. Al listened to the silence and the sound of his heart pounding in his temples. The plane jolted, and there was a loud thump and bang at the front, like they had hit something.

"Ladies and gentlemen, this is your captain again. We've landed safely, and we're sorry for the inconvenience. The ground crew and mechanics will be looking over our plane to see if they can make the necessary repairs. We're going to ask that you de-plane and wait in the terminal for further instructions."

Al heard a noise in his lap, and the seat belt separated and fell to each side. He was relieved to be free but was trying to process what had just happened. He hadn't heard or felt them land on the runway, and the whole sequence of events was unnerving. Maybe he had fallen asleep or maybe he just wasn't feeling well. He thought about it as he got up from his seat and stepped over and into the aisle. He looked back to see the other passengers doing the same. In the ten aisles behind him there were five other passengers, and that was it. That didn't make sense either. He turned back around and walked to the front of the plane.

As he reached the exit, the door to the pilot's bridge swung open.

The flight attendant stepped out. "Mr. Cohen, please follow me," she said to him, pointing toward the open hatch door.

Al stepped forward and stuck his head into the bridge where the pilot was.

"Uh, thank you—I think. Where are we?" he said to the back of the pilot's head.

The pilot turned around. "Mr. Cohen, the flight attendant will show you to the waiting area and will answer all of your questions." Then he said, "Adiós, amigo."

Al detected a hint of sarcasm in the pilot's voice. He also thought he heard the man chuckle. As Al turned, he saw the co-pilot sitting at a side table in front of a full instrument panel. The young man had a silly grin on his face but said nothing.

Al shook his head and followed the flight attendant out the hatch down and onto a platform leading to an enclosed hallway. The walls were sterile-white and rose up to a curved ceiling. Unusually bright light illuminated the hallway, from no apparent source.

"Watch your step, Mr. Cohen," she said as she grabbed Al by the arm and led him onto a moving walkway.

Al stepped on, wobbled, then regained his footing.

The moving walkway went on for about twenty meters and ended at another stationary platform. They both stepped on to the platform.

"Mr. Cohen, for the safety of all the passengers, we'll have each of you depart individually," the attendant said.

In front of them the wall slid open, revealing a closet-sized room.

The flight attendant still had Al by the arm, and she nudged him forward. "Mr. Cohen, please step in."

Al stepped in. He turned his head and saw the wall close up behind him. He looked forward again at another blank, white wall. The pounding in his temples returned, and he could hear nothing else.

After a minute the wall in front of him slid open. The piercing white light coming through the door burned his eyes. He raised his hand to cover them. The floor he was standing on began to move slowly, and Al didn't know what to do. His feet shuffled, but he maintained his balance and a firm footing.

The floor moved him out of the closet and into another room. The heat in this room slammed against him. The bright light seeped through his fingers and his eyelids. He could see only white and feel only heat. He wondered if this was the light people see when life comes to an end.

Then the floor stopped moving.

"Hey, what's going on?" Al was scared, and his fear was evident in his cracking voice.

There was no response.

"I demand to know what's going on," he yelled. "I have rights!"

Again, there was no response.

Al stood motionless, waiting, listening, unable to see anything. He was a blind man in a completely foreign world with nobody, with nothing, to help him. He had never been so scared in his life.

Suddenly, the floor under him began to move again. This time it spun him slowly clockwise. It was all he could do to maintain his footing. He wanted to speak, wanted to yell, but nothing came. His brain could not process what was happening, so no words were available.

Around and around and around he went.

After a short time, the lights seemed to dim ever so slightly. Al lowered his hands and opened his eyes a crack, still squinting. He let his eyes adjust to the light. While still blinding, it was getting more tolerable. The lights dimmed further, and he looked around as he spun.

He was in a large, glass-enclosed room. As he continued to spin, he saw only darkened glass and nothing beyond. He made one full rotation and noticed there was someone else in the room with him. He shielded his eyes and strained to look. Five meters away, he saw another man, standing on a white platform attached to a rail, the same rail to which Al's platform was attached. The man's platform was spinning just like his, and the man stood there fixed and frozen, obviously terrified and wondering what the hell was going on.

More and more was coming into focus now. Al looked beyond the man next to him and saw another man on a similar pedestal-floor, and beyond him was another man, and another. In all, there were six men, each on their own moving platform, floors rotating as though they were on display. Al saw the same fear and rigidity in each of the men as they turned.

He thought it unusual that no one was saying anything. They were as silent as he was. No one dared move for fear of falling off the platform. He looked down and around, and saw nothing but darkness.

He also noticed that all the other men glistened in the same unusual way. It looked like they had bathed in baby oil, and the lights shone on them and displayed their tanned skin in a flattering way. Al felt his forehead and remembered the oil he had applied.

The silence was suddenly broken with a flurry of foreign sounds. Al struggled to determine their nature, but they were unlike anything he had ever heard before. They were cackles, sharp and throaty, in a variety of pitches. Some were screeched at a fever pitch that hurt his ears. Others were in lower tones, and all were distinctly different. He could not tell exactly where the sounds were coming from, but they did not seem to be coming from inside the room. They were coming from behind the glass, and if he didn't know any better, he would swear it was some form of communication. In addition to the strange cackling sounds, Al heard muffled murmurs. He listened intently and thought he heard someone on the other side of the glass speaking his language. He couldn't be sure.

The men continued to rotate on their platforms, their feet firmly planted as though in cement. They turned, they glistened, and they smelled.

Finally, a man at the far end yelled, "LET ME OUT OF HERE!"

Then the floodgates opened, and each of the men began shouting, releasing their fears and frustrations. Some swore. Some pleaded. One man was sobbing uncontrollably and could say nothing. Al joined in. An endless stream of expletives rang out, words and sayings coming from deep within the darkest part of him. The yelling from the men could not compete with the cackling from the other side of the glass, but they didn't care.

Then Al noticed one of the glass walls begin to move. The lights intensified, and he could no longer see through the blinding white. The cackling entered his room through the open glass, and it was almost deafening. But he could also now hear more clearly the words of an English-speaking man. The man was yelling, but Al could not understand what he was saying. It sounded like an argument, but he

171

could not make out the details.

The volume of the cackling intensified, and Al thought his eardrums were going to explode. He heard cries of terror and pain coming from some of the other men, and he raised his hands to cover his ears.

He could not see and could not hear. The heat burned his skin, and he could smell and taste it in the air.

The cackling ceased.

Fearful, Al lowered his hands. What he heard next nearly stopped his heart.

"But that one's not ready," he heard through the open glass wall.

A shadow moved over Al, blocking the piercing white light. He opened his eyes. Through slits he saw something coming toward him, a large claw-like apparition. He shook away the dream he thought he was having and tried to make sense of what he was seeing.

The two scaly-green tendrils came down and wrapped around him. He tried to scream, but the constricting pressure around his chest prevented that. He felt himself levitate off the platform and into the air. He spun around, rose, spun, rose. All his muscles tightened, then relaxed as gases and fluids escaped.

The last sound he heard was the crunching of bones.

NOTES ON
ADIÓS AMIGO

The idea for the story *Adiós Amigo* came to me as I was sitting with my family in the international airport in Guadalajara, Mexico. It was the first week in January 2008, and we were returning from a holiday vacation. We were tired and dripping with sweat as we sat, as still as possible, waiting for our plane home to board. I made an observation and subsequent comment to my daughter, who was sitting next to me. We looked out the mile-high windows and saw the distant runways, and the magnified sun beat down upon us. I asked her, somewhat rhetorically, if it could be any hotter. She just looked at me and sweated. I wondered, aloud, if maybe someone, or something, might be intentionally trying to cook us, for it very much felt like we were sitting in an oven. Perspiring and just wanting to go home, she shrugged with an expression of *maybe*.

Back in my office a week later, as I sat at my desk in a small room above a La Grange storefront, the story started to take shape. The airport scene became a turning point for the story. I had an idea of how to get the characters to the airport and I knew that once there, their lives would be changed forever.

The protagonist, Al Cohen, and his wife, Margie, are characters everyone can identify with. In them, one can feel compassion,

173

sympathy, empathy, and maybe even a little disgust. They are not perfect. They are just regular people, possibly more regular than you think. You may not like a character like Al, but you can understand who he is, where he came from, and the predicament he is in. Margie, unfortunately, is largely a victim of circumstance, which is also quite understandable.

Adiós Amigo brings together a personal experience, a love for science fiction, and what I feel—and what I hope for the reader—is an original and interesting ending. The ending was there at the start; I just needed to figure out how to get there. I had a vague idea of what Al was going to be like, but he really developed, as did Margie, as the story progressed. That's one of the great beauties of writing a story: it is as much a journey for the writer as it is for the characters and the reader. It's only through the story that the journey can take place, and this one was quite a journey.

It was great fun to write this story and it provided a few comic moments. I chuckled at times as I wrote the story and I can still remember reading it to my son, tears dripping down my face while trying to get the words out. I laughed hard and cried, likely thinking something more clever than it was. As I read the story, he just laughed because I laughed, and that is just as good.

There is something to be said about writing for your own pleasure. Naturally, every writer wants to write a story that another person finds enjoyable. However, I do not think there is much chance of gaining a large audience if the story does not resonate initially with the writer. This story resonates with me, for some strange reason, and although I have likely read it a dozen times, I still like it and it still makes me laugh. I love being a writer.

In the end, I think this story would make a great *Twilight Zone* episode. I'm a big fan of the show. I hope some day the series gets another shot and is brought back to life, or a new series like it is created. I will be the first in line to pitch an episode. Maybe I'll just put the creation of a *Twilight Zone*-like television series on my "to do" list and make it happen.

Until then, I don't think I can ever look at a chicken the same way again.

An Unexpected Guest
– *A Fantasy*

I pulled into the garage, delighted that another workday had ended. More and more, I was looking forward to the end of the business day, and the desire to reach it was occurring to me earlier and earlier in the mornings, so that I was getting the feeling as I left the house for the office.

The consulting business I started thirteen years ago was still doing extremely well, but I had lost the passion for it. My daily routine, while always different in its details, had overall become a monotonous exercise in business and personnel management. More often than not, it seemed like babysitting, and my patience was wearing thin. I always said I would continue with the business as long as it was fun, but the fun had run out on me years ago.

I had met with my two partners several months back and shared with them my desire to sell my stock in the company and step away from the business. With respect to my partners, nothing ever happened quickly, so the process of finalizing the purchase agreement and my retirement date dragged on. By now it was all I could do to get up every morning to go into the office. The end was near, but I was not sure how near.

Although I talked about retirement, I was not of retirement age.

I had been incredibly fortunate in obtaining a solid education, having many influential business and personal mentors, and getting into a very lucrative industry. However, at forty-four years of age, I had come to the end of my second career, and I knew I still had several more careers to pursue. Now seemed the time to get the next one going.

I turned off the engine, sat for a moment, and enjoyed the silence. I always loved coming home at the end of the day. My wife and children were always there with smiling faces and open arms, ready to tell me all about the day's happenings.

I especially looked forward to getting home today for my birthday dinner. For the most part, birthdays come and go as most other days. I always tried to make my birthday as uneventful as possible. If I could be with my family for dinner and have a little birthday cake, I was happy. Handmade cards from my wife and children are the gifts I keep forever and cherish the most.

The topic of my birthday scarcely came up during the day. I received the obligatory birthday card, signed by all of the office staff. I also received a smattering of emails and voice messages from those family members and friends that never forget a birthday, which I cherished as well.

I grabbed my briefcase, got out of the car, and walked up the steps to the front door. Inside, my daughter and son were the first to greet me. We hugged, kissed, and hugged again. I asked if they had a good day at school, and they asked if I had a good day at work. They said "yes," and I believed them. I said "yes," but I was beginning to think they could see right through me. I tried to be positive and cheerful, but I think they knew I was not enjoying my work as I had in the past.

The children broke away and cleared a path for their mother. I went to her, and we embraced, a strong, loving embrace with a "Hi" and "I love you" in each ear. We walked to the kitchen, hand-in-hand, and I asked her about her day. I got the highlights, and as she talked I stopped at the refrigerator to grab a beer. I sat down at the kitchen table, took a few sips, and listened intently. When she finished, she looked at me and smiled, knowing better than to ask me about my day. I had given her the same daily report ever since I notified my business partners of my wish to retire. She supported me fully and looked forward to my retirement date.

I asked her about dinner, and she told me she had a surprise for me. She had prepared my favorite dish and said a special guest was joining us for dinner. I did not say anything, but she could tell from my expression that I was not happy about the idea. We had dinner guests every once in a while, but it was usually on the weekend up at the lake house. I was generally in a very different frame of mind on the weekend, and I really enjoyed cooking and entertaining guests. During the week, I did not have the heart for it. Especially on my birthday, she knew I did not want to have to entertain and that I was not interested in any type of birthday party.

I could feel my facial expression changing, and as my wife stared, I shared some non-verbal communication that she understood clearly. My face said to her, "oh no," then "not tonight," then "I'm really not in the mood for this." She told me not to worry, that it really was a big surprise and that she was sure I would enjoy the evening.

A very old friend of mine just happened to be in the neighborhood, she explained, and was stopping by. I really could not imagine who it might be, but before I could say anything, she continued, sharing some clues because she knew I was clueless. She said I would recognize *him* instantly. *Well, that's a good start,* I thought. She went further to say it was someone I was very close to, whom I admired and deeply respected. She added that I had not seen this man in quite some time, and it all became perfectly clear—perfectly clear that I had absolutely no idea who she was talking about. Anyone meeting that description—my father or my first business mentor— had passed away years ago.

The only person I could think of was my old pal, Steven Halloway. We were close friends and football comrades in grade school, wrestling foes in high school, and roommates in college. I was the best man at his wedding and he at mine. Unfortunately, the life changes that come with starting a career and a family take considerable effort and time, and time we used to spend together hanging out instead went to getting the next promotion and going to the kids' soccer games. He was one of those rare individuals with whom you always knew where you stood. We based our friendship on loyalty, and no matter how long the gap in our visits, when we got together it was as if I had just seen him the day before. I probably had not seen him in seven or eight years, yet I could picture him in my mind clear as day.

It's funny how your mood can change in an instant. With a smile on my face, I rose from my chair and shouted my guess to my wife. She looked back at me first with a *you just might have it* expression, followed quickly by *close-but-no-cigar*. She told me Steven would not be joining us, and there would be no more guessing. Our mystery guest would be arriving in about half an hour, and she had some final arrangements to take care of. She got another beer from the refrigerator, set it in front of me, and told me to relax. I offered to help, but she quickly held up a hand, palm facing me, and dismissed that suggestion. I did not fight it and instead took another few sips from my beer.

She had enlisted the children to help her, and I watched them as they ran back and forth from the kitchen to the dining room, carrying plates, silverware, and glasses. The small television in the kitchen was on, replaying the day's news events. I didn't bother to listen. The never-ending stream of negativity, horror, and biased viewpoint channeled through the television airwaves had no part in my life. The stereo in the living room was on as well, playing random tracks from my extensive jazz collection. I turned off the TV so I could better hear the music.

There was a fantastic aroma swirling around the kitchen, coming from a large pot on the stove. I could pinpoint that smell from a mile away. It was my favorite red sauce, a family recipe passed down from my mother and enhanced over the years. The current incarnation of the recipe was most certainly our own, and I sometimes joked (or maybe I was serious) that we could open an Italian restaurant based only on the merits of our sauce.

My wife mentioned earlier that she was preparing my favorite dish, simple angel hair pasta with red sauce. Add a side of meatballs and a decent bottle of red wine, and I could not be happier. Over the years, I have judged many, if not most, of the Italian restaurants I have visited based upon their ability to serve a good red sauce. A good red sauce is dazzling in its simplicity, yet requires the perfect matching of quality tomatoes, spices, and a few secret ingredients. Not everyone can prepare a decent sauce, but my wife sure could, and I knew I would enjoy it.

My wife called from the dining room, asking if I could open the wine on the counter. I got up and walked over to find three bottles of one of my favorite cabernets. *Three bottles?* I thought, *this is going to be some dinner party* and wondered who else was coming. Either we were having more than one guest, or we were shooting for inebriation. I opened a bottle, smelled the cork, and wondered why I did that. I did not like the smell of cork, and I really could not tell anything about the wine by it.

As I set down the cork and put the corkscrew back in the drawer, the doorbell rang. My daughter said she would get it, and her younger brother ran after her to try to beat her to the door. From the kitchen, I heard the front door open, followed by some brief conversation too soft for me to understand. My wife joined the children at the door, and the conversation continued. "There's someone here to see you," she said.

The mystery guest, I thought, and headed to the front door. Halfway through the living room, I tucked my shirt in and looked down to make sure I was presentable. Then I looked up to see who was at the door and stopped dead in my tracks.

Standing before me was most certainly the person my wife had described earlier: a man I admired and respected, had a strong connection to, and who I had not seen in quite a few years. There in the doorway stood Ray Bradbury.

A wave of emotions raced through my brain and body. In an instant, a multitude of questions presented themselves, received no answer, and fled. *What was Ray Bradbury doing in La Grange, Illinois, and what was he doing at my house? Who called him? Was he really here to see me? Why do I feel feverish, and why am I sweating? Am I going to stand frozen in this spot forever, or am I going to snap out of it and not be such a dork?*

I blurted out a subtle "Oh my," and walked to the door to welcome our guest. I extended my hand to say hello. We shook hands, while I said, "Ray, what a pleasant surprise. Please come in, and welcome to our home."

Ray said, "I understand this is a special day for you, birthday boy." He seemed to giggle a little bit as he said it, like a kid up to no good.

I looked at him quizzically. His expression reminded me of a small child who had kept a secret from his friend for a month and had just let it loose. His face reflected delight, excitement, and relief that the secret was finally out. I heard him giggle again.

He said to me, "I really do love your front hallway here, but do you think I might be able to come in?"

"Absolutely!" I said, as I snapped out of my trance.

Ray turned around and called out to a man who was standing on our front porch, "Patrick, I'll be all right. I'll call you when I'm ready to leave."

The man he referred to as Patrick was Ray's driver and personal assistant. He wore a nicely tailored suit and dark sunglasses, and held Ray's wheelchair folded up. I could tell he was wondering if Ray might want it or need it. Before he could ask, Ray spoke.

"I won't be needing that this evening, Patrick. I think it will just get in the way."

Patrick nodded and turned to descend the stairs so he could go back to the car.

I said, "Patrick, why don't you come in and join us?"

He replied, "Thank you, but I have some errands to run." He said to Ray, "Just call when you're ready, and I'll be here."

We all watched as he walked down the stairs to the car, loaded the wheelchair in the trunk, got into the driver's seat, and pulled away.

Another chuckle came from Ray. "Yeah, he sure does have some errands to run, the first one being a stop at the McDonald's we passed on our way here. The boy loves his Big Mac."

Without asking, Ray grabbed my arm. We walked into the living room, past my wife and children. They stood there in a line, each with a smiling face and sparkling eyes. They knew they had just pulled off the impossible—surprising Dad on his birthday with a gift that would never be outdone or forgotten. I smiled back at each of them, like a kid on Christmas morning.

My wife suggested we sit in the living room, but Ray asked if it would be all right if we just went to the dining room table. His legs were not what they used to be, he said, and he thought it would be better to walk and sit once. He also commented that something smelled great, and he wanted to be well prepared when dinner came.

We walked to the dining room, and I motioned to him to sit at the head of the table. "You're the birthday boy," he insisted. "Just sit me here right next to you, and I'll be fine." I helped him into his chair and scooted him in. Without hesitation, the rest of the family took their seats.

A second later, my wife was up again, running off to the kitchen to put the final touches on dinner. My children just sat there, looking at Ray with huge, silly grins. Ray looked back at them with a silly grin of his own.

"How about a drink?" I said.

"How about some wine?" Ray asked.

"Can we have some soda?" the children asked in unison.

"We just happen to have one of my favorite red wines, special for this evening," I said.

"Three bottles?" Ray asked.

How did he know that?

Ray said, "I hope you don't mind, but at my age, one of my last great pleasures in life is enjoying a fine red wine, and it's good for the heart, you know? When I talked with your wife about the arrangements for this evening, I asked her about your favorite wine and had three bottles sent over. Will that be enough?"

"It will be a good start," I said and excused myself to get our drinks.

I returned moments later with a tray that included the open bottle of wine, three wine glasses, and two glasses of Sprite for the children. I served the soft drinks, set down the wine glasses, and poured the wine. Then I sat down and grabbed my glass.

"Honey, come on in and join us for a toast," I shouted.

She hurried into the dining room, grabbed her glass, and remained standing behind her chair.

I raised my glass and said, "To our very special guest. Ray, welcome to our home. I still can't believe you're here, but you're always welcome. Feel free to stop by any time, really."

I raised my glass to my lips, but Ray reached out to stop me.

"Not so fast. I have something I want to say." He raised his own glass. "It is my pleasure to be here with you on your special day. Your wife went to great lengths to track me down and get in contact with me, and she is a great persuader. When I heard about your love for my books, your passion for writing, and all the great things you have said about me, I had no choice but to come and see you. I believe we are kindred spirits, and I am grateful for the opportunity to share this time with you. May you have the most cherished of birthdays, and may you be successful in all that you do."

We all raised our glasses.

"Live forever!" he shouted and clinked his glass with mine. A subsequent flurry of clinking ensued around the table, and when the clinking stopped, we drank.

I knew the source of Ray's exclamation, *"Live Forever."* Those were the words Mr. Electrico, the magician, said to Ray when he was a twelve-year-old boy at a circus he visited many years ago. I had read about that encounter several times in various biographies, including *The Bradbury Chronicles.* In that book he said, "I decided that was the greatest idea I ever heard. Just weeks after Mr. Electrico said that to me, I started writing every day, and I never stopped."

I loved the idea as well. Not only should we live with the belief that we may live forever, but we should also try to live each day as though it were the most important one. Live each day as though it might be your last. That interpretation had driven me in my work, my writing, and my relationship with my family.

"So, I understand you want to be a writer, eh?" Ray inquired.

"I *am* a writer," I replied.

Ray threw his head back and laughed, a laugh from deep down within him that made his whole body jiggle. "Excellent! That's wonderful!"

His reaction surprised me. "What?"

"You are, you are a writer. I can see it in your eyes and hear it in your voice. I can already tell you write from your heart. Do that, add a good dose of passion and perseverance, and you'll be remarkably successful."

I told him of my love for books and my dream to be a writer. The dream was ten years in the making, and I had just recently made the commitment to turn it into a reality. Ray smiled as I shared my plans with him, and he understood my passion. He'd had the same boundless determination as a young writer.

"I've even written a few short stories," I said.

He continued to smile and drank his wine.

"I wouldn't want to impose, but I'm not sure when I'll ever have the opportunity again. Maybe after dinner you could read one of my stories and tell me what you think."

"Why wait?" he replied. "We probably have a little time before dinner. Go get me one of your stories, and if it's all right with everyone else, I'll read it right now."

He looked at the children, and they nodded their approval. I quickly got up, ran to my office, and grabbed the story I had just finished: *The Pass*. It was about a man's encounter with fate, his struggle to understand and deal with a real-life miracle, and his belief in the good of humanity. I ran back to the table and offered the manuscript to Ray. He reached for it eagerly and began to read. I sat down, and the children and I watched him as he scanned the pages. I looked for any signal, any sign of acknowledgement, pleasure, or dissatisfaction in his expression as he read. His eyes darted back and forth, and he turned the pages hungrily.

I grew uneasy as he read. There, sitting at my dinner table, was one of the greatest authors of all time, and he was reading one of my stories. What if he hated it? What if it was pure dreck? Here I had put him in a position to comment on my writing, and now I was not sure I wanted to hear what he might say. My shirt collar felt a little tight, and beads of perspiration formed on my forehead. I reached for my wine and finished it. I grabbed the bottle and refilled my glass, and then I leaned over to refill Ray's empty glass as well. He grabbed it, raised it to his lips, and took a long swallow. I did the same.

It was getting almost too much to bear. He had been flipping pages for some time, and I could see he was coming to the end of the story. I looked at my children, who had sat quietly and watched intently as Ray read. My son turned to me, raised his eyebrows, and jutted his chin in Ray's direction. He wanted me to look.

I looked back at Ray. He was at the last page. I watched as the corners of his mouth turned upward and his eyes grew wide. A smile seemed to take up half of his face, while a tear welled in the corner of his left eye and floated down his cheek. He set down the manuscript and wiped at his eyes with his napkin.

"That is a fine story," he said.

I almost fell off my chair. "Do you really think so?"

"Absolutely. There is great conflict, good plot movement, and good resolution. Most important, you wrote it with feeling and passion. I'd guess that some of what you wrote you've actually experienced, and that's a sign of a good writer—someone who has the ability to capture the feelings and emotions of experience and weave them into a fictional story."

Ray took up his glass again. "You are indeed a writer," he said. He clinked his glass with mine, and we drank.

"Hey, don't leave us out," my son said, and we brought our glasses together with theirs.

My wife came into the room carrying a covered dish. "What did I miss?" she asked.

"You have nothing to worry about. Your husband is a fine writer and is off to a great start," Ray said.

She smiled, then looked at me, and smiled even bigger. She set down the dish and rested her hands on her hips. "Well, that's great to hear, but it's something I already knew." She winked at me. "Is anybody hungry? I think we're just about ready to eat."

Over the next hour, we ate, drank, and talked about everything under the sun. Ray took a particular interest in the children, and we talked about their favorite books, favorite subjects at school, and what they most liked about being a kid. Ray shared the many things *he* liked about being a kid.

After we cleared the table, we settled in for some dessert. As we passed the birthday cake around, Ray said to the children, "I bet you didn't know this, but I knew your Grandpa."

"Really?" my daughter said.

"No way," my son added.

"It's true," Ray replied, and he looked at me for a reaction.

I tried to read his face and could not. I just assumed he was embarking on a little good-natured storytelling.

"You don't believe me?" Ray said, directing his question to me.

"Oh, I believe you," I said, going along with the ruse and interested in what was to come.

Ray had hooked the children, and they sat up straight in their chairs and listened carefully. Even my wife was intrigued.

"Well, as some of you know, I grew up in Waukegan, which is a town not too far from here and just north of Chicago. Your Grandpa grew up in the city, and I had a chance to meet him when I was a young boy. We met at a birthday party for a mutual friend, and while at the party we found we were both there alone—with our friends but still isolated. We forged a bond that day, and we remained friends through the years.

"We were different in many ways, as most children are, but we were also very much alike. We were both children of the Great Depression. Kids, did you learn about that in school?"

They acknowledged that they had and added what they remembered about that troubled time in American history.

Ray continued, "The Great Depression started with the stock market crash of 1929 and was the longest and most severe economic depression in the history of the Western world. It had a profound impact on our values and beliefs. During the following ten-year period, banks failed, people lost everything, and unemployment was at an all-time high. It was a very stressful and trying time for the American people."

I had heard family stories about my grandfather's struggles during that time, as he pursued various jobs to keep his family clothed and fed. At one point, he was even a private investigator.

Ray continued, "We were both the youngest children in our family, and our ages separated us sufficiently from our siblings so that we could pursue our own interests. I was interested in books and going to the library. I was also interested in cutting out and collecting comic strips from the newspaper. Did you know your Grandpa had one of the finest collections of Buck Rogers comic strips?"

The children shook their heads, and my wife and I did as well. It was funny. I really could not say what my father's interests were as a young child. For all I knew, he did have a great collection of comics.

Ray looked at me as he continued.

"During the Depression, our fathers had difficulty finding and keeping work, which meant money was tight. There were few extravagances, and we learned to amuse ourselves and create our own fun. We learned at a young age the value of hard work, the value of a dollar, and the importance of family. I can say with utmost certainty that you learned these same values from your father, which is why you are successful and have such a wonderful family."

I smiled and acknowledged the fact without having to say a word.

"We traded frequent letters over the years up until World War II. Your father *was* in the service, yes?" he asked.

"He was," I replied. "He left high school after his junior year and enlisted in the Navy. He was a firefighter, first class, and an electrician. He served thirty months and spent most of his time on a LST, a land shore tank; the kind of boat that pulled right up to shore with the troops and let them off through the end of the boat that dropped down onto the shore."

"Your father was a brave man," he said to me. "I was terrified of the war. I knew that if I went to war, I would never come home. I struggled with my fears for years, but I finally registered for the draft. When my time came to go in for my physical, they said I was blind as a bat without my glasses and classified me as physically ineligible to serve. I was lucky, and I was allowed to stay home and continue to work on my writing."

He turned to the children. "Kids, your grandpa went to war to serve his country and protect everything that makes our country great. Your grandpa was a real American hero. Don't you ever forget that."

The war was one of those topics that our family never discussed. As a young boy, I remember asking my father about his time in the Navy, and he answered every question. However, I learned quickly that it was a topic he would rather not discuss. He kept his war very private, stored away in a deep, dark place inside of him where he could manage and deal with it.

As Ray talked, it occurred to me how much he resembled my father. A couple of years back, I had the opportunity to meet Ray in San Diego after a speech he gave, and I remember how he looked sitting there on stage in his wheelchair. Like my father, he had a full head of hair, albeit completely white and slightly disheveled. They both also wore large eyeglasses, and they had many similar mannerisms. They dressed the same, and Ray even looked through his eyeglasses with the same half-open mouth and inquisitive expression. When I returned home from that trip, I mentioned to my wife the uncanny similarities. Now, as he sat close at the table, I felt that my father was there with me.

"During the fifties, big cars were all the rage," Ray went on. "Did you know that I never learned to drive and have never owned a car?"

The children looked at him with an odd expression, as if wondering if he was from this planet.

"How did you get around?" my son asked.

"Oh, I learned to love the fine art of walking. I walked everywhere. I bet your grandfather walked all the time as a young man."

"Eighteen blocks each way to get to school, even in the rain and snow," I added. My father had made sure to remind me of that fact at least a thousand times.

"As I got older, I was fortunate that other people were available to drive me around and make sure I got to where I was supposed to be. Patrick, my current driver and good friend, has been taking care of me now for just about forever," Ray said.

He paused to take a breath and a drink. Then he turned to me again. "Your father worked hard and saved his money for many years, then treated himself to one of those fine automobiles, didn't he?"

"He sure did. His first car was a 1955 Chevy Bel Air Coupe," I said.

"That was one beautiful car," Ray replied. "I remember they came with a combination color scheme, with some of the most unbelievable colors ever to be put on an automobile."

I knew what he meant and added, "His came off the line with an incredible coral and gray paint job. I wish they would make those cars again."

"And I bet you and your father had a very close relationship. You were probably inseparable when you were young, then drifted apart some when you went away to college, began your career, and started a family. In the end, your relationship came full circle, and you were best friends again in the years before he died. And the best thing of all, you're getting to re-live the relationship with your father through your relationship with your children."

He paused, then added, "You are a fine gentleman and a lucky man. Happy birthday and may you have many more."

We raised our glasses for a toast and I reached up to wipe my watery eyes.

"Thank you. Thank you, Ray, for coming to spend time with me. And honey, kids, thank you for the best birthday present ever."

"Well, I have to be leaving soon," Ray said. "I can't keep Patrick waiting for too long, and my pillow awaits me. But before I leave, I would love to see this collection of my books that I've heard so much about."

"It would be my honor," I said as I rose from my chair. "Would you all excuse us for a moment?"

"If you wouldn't mind giving me a hand up, I'll just hold onto your arm," Ray said.

"My office is just down the hall."

He gripped my arm tightly as we walked into my office, and I led him to a comfortable leather chair in the corner. Directly across from him was a glass-door bookcase, filled to over-flowing with books.

I gestured toward it. "This is my collection of signed volumes, and this right-hand section is everything I have written by and signed by you."

"Well, to say I'm flattered is an understatement. Which one is your favorite?" he asked.

I reached into the top shelf and pulled out a copy of *Dandelion Wine*. "This is my favorite book of yours. I picked up this copy a couple of years ago. It's a first edition, in near-perfect condition. The only problem is, the title page is blank—no signature." I grinned and raised my eyebrows a couple of times. He started to laugh.

"Give that to me, and hand me a pen."

I handed him the book. I hurried to my desk, pulled a pen from the top drawer, and handed it to him as well.

He opened the book, clicked the pen, and scribbled furiously for just a few seconds, then closed the book and set it down on the reading table next to him. "You can look at that later. Help me up and let's give Patrick a ring."

I helped him up, and we walked back into the living room. Patrick was there at the door. My wife must have read our minds, as she had called him once we left the table. She stood at the door with the children right beside her. Ray said goodbye to the children first, and they both hugged him. He thanked my wife, leaned over, and whispered something in her ear. She giggled. Then he turned to me. "Well, birthday boy, get over here and say goodbye."

I went to him, and we shook hands. I moved closer, hugged him, and kissed him on the cheek. "Thank you," I said.

"It was my pleasure," he replied. He turned, grabbed onto Patrick's arm, and walked out the door.

We followed him out onto the front porch and watched until he was in the car. As they drove away, we waved, saying goodbye again without speaking.

Later that evening, after we finished the dishes and the children were in bed, I went back to my office to straighten up a bit. As I walked in, I noticed the copy of *Dandelion Wine* on my reading table where I left it. I sat down in the chair and picked up the book. I opened it to the title page and read what Ray had written.

To Dan,

Zest! Gusto! Love! Hatred! Excitement! Without these feelings, you're only half a writer.

You're going to be great!

Ray Bradbury

I closed the book, rested it in my lap, and smiled.

NOTES ON
AN UNEXPECTED GUEST
– A FANTASY

I read a lot of periodicals related to writing. As I do with books, I tend to get more magazines than I can possibly read in a lifetime. I don't care. I love receiving the writing magazines in the mail, and I keep them stacked and filed in my office. Some day I'll get to them and who knows when I might need to refer to one for a project I'm working on.

My approach to reading magazines was instilled in me at an early age. As a young boy, I can remember asking my mother if I could get a subscription to my favorite magazine, *Popular Mechanics*. Money was tight at the time, but she agreed with one condition: that I promise to read at least one article from each issue. Her rationale was that if I read one article, that was one article more than I would have read otherwise, and she would invest any amount of money to get me to read more. It was a deal, and I've been doing my best to follow that promise ever since.

In October of 2007, I was scanning an issue of *Writer's Digest* that was collecting dust on my desk. It was the April 2007 issue, and I came across a writing prompt that intrigued me. I wrote the prompt down, modified it slightly, and sat back in my chair as I pondered the premise for my next story: *On my birthday, instead of buying me a present, my wife announced that she had invited a mystery guest for dinner.*

I don't usually rely on writing prompts to get me going, but I'll take a good idea wherever I can get one. Coming up with the mystery guest was the easy part. It was my fictional birthday and my fantasy, and I wanted to have dinner with the one person who prompted me to embark on my new career as a writer, the one who gave me the nudge I needed. He was the one person who had the biggest influence on my writing career, then and now: Ray Bradbury.

Often, personal experience makes its way into a writer's story. It's only natural. At the time I wrote this story, I was putting an end to a prior chapter in my life. I was parting ways with my business partner of fifteen years and a friend for much longer. While initially we agreed to work through the dissolution and finalize the arrangements civilly, ending a business partnership and a friendship is never that easy. To say I was a little stressed out would be an understatement. Anyway, I was certain that a fictional birthday dinner with my family and Ray Bradbury was just the encounter I needed to put me in the right frame of mind.

I got to work and pounded out the story in one sitting, almost as though it was happening in real time. It was a fine dinner we had, and given Ray's influence on my career, it seemed only fitting to include the story in my first short story collection.

This one is for you, Ray.

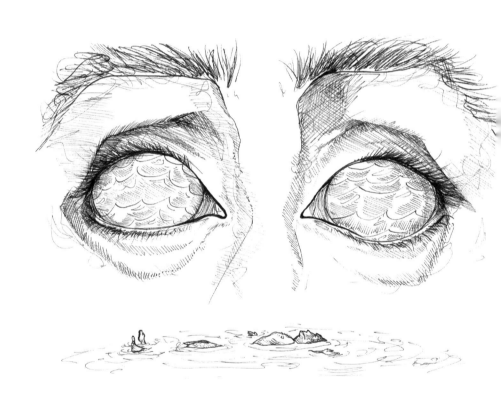

THE PASS

The adrenaline pumped through his veins like a raging locomotive, each revolution of its circular metal wheels creating a pounding and pulsing sensation in his temples. Each of his senses was on alert, and at the same time, an uneasy feeling that he might be out of control swept over him. Rational thought was gone, and pure animal instinct took over. Cool beads of sweat formed on his sunburned forehead, and upon reaching their full weight, they began their descent. Some of the salty droplets caught on his furry brows that created a deliberate ridge, while some made it through the opening at the bridge of the nose and rolled down its slope. It was hot outside, but his internal temperature escalated rapidly to an unsafe level.

He found his hands steering the boat in the right direction, yet he had no thoughts about direction or speed. The boat was full, yet he could not hear the unsettled and concerned voices of the passengers. He focused his complete attention on the water in front of him and off the right side of the boat. He tried to process the scene unfolding, and his adrenaline and blood-engorged brain struggled for an explanation. After a long moment, he saw it more clearly. A man was floating in the water, vested but face down. His jet ski was just a few yards from him, circling and waiting for him to return. He would not be returning.

Rick Bradley was completely alone, as was the young man, who floated and bobbed in the water like a beacon.

Rick brought the boat to its final destination, shifted the throttle into reverse, and cut the engine. The vessel rocked gently on the wakes from the passing boats and settled into a calm, swaying motion. The exhaust from the engine back-drafted into the cabin area, and it stung his eyes and burned his nostrils.

Some unknown force within him took over. In seconds, he had left the captain's station and was standing on the top edge of the right side of the boat. Past training as a lifeguard should have told him to make a rescuer's leap so he could keep his target in full sight. Instead, he dove in headfirst. The dive followed a horizontal plane, much like the pistol-start dive at a swimming race. His hands hit first, then his head, and the rest of his body followed, cutting through the water like a torpedo. His head remained under for just seconds and stayed mere inches under the surface. While under, he opened his eyes and could see only darkness. The crisp, cool water against heated skin sent a shock to his heart. His body tensed, relaxed, and then tensed again. Only one thought raced through his mind.

I hope he is not dead.

Somehow, Rick Bradley covered the distance between the man and the boat with surprising ease. His head broke the surface, and he inhaled the cool mist coming off the water. He opened his eyes and kept them open as the water cleared, and he could see that the man was right in front of him. His lifeless body floated with the waves, riding each as it crested and following the slope down into the depression left behind. His head and shoulders were in front of Rick, his face down as if he were blindly searching the depths of the lake. Rick grabbed him by the shoulders and turned him over. The man's face was a pallid bluish gray, tight, cold, and devoid of life. Rick's earlier thought gave way to one that signaled his brain to trigger his stomach muscles, which tightened. Stomach acid began to flow freely, and the nausea hit him.

Oh God, I hope the children can't see this.

An hour earlier, they had boarded the boat for a short afternoon excursion. Rick's best friends, Tom and Carol Anderson, arrived in the morning and were joining him and Linda for a weekend at their lake house. Alex and Abbey, the Andersons' twin six-year-old girls, had talked for weeks about going boating and tubing, and it was time to hit the water. The girls and Caitlin, Rick and Linda's young daughter, sat in the open bow area, talking and playing. Tom and Carol sat in the rear section with Rick and Linda, enjoying light conversation and catching up on the latest happenings since they last saw each other.

The excursion began with a cruise around the perimeter of the lake, taking in the sights and sounds of life on the water and the scenes playing out on the surrounding shorelines. It was later in the season, but the water was surprisingly warm, which meant the lake was still full of recreational boaters. These weekend captains of the open water had their engines at full throttle, pulling skis or a tube for the ride of a lifetime. Jet skis followed in their wakes, staying dangerously close to the passing boats to catch the best waves. Any conformance to boaters' etiquette or appropriate lane usage was disregarded as the watercraft crisscrossed in a careless and random manner.

Rick decided to stay away from the commotion for the time being and rode close to the shoreline. He kept the engine's throttle just above idle, and they cruised the mild waters as they viewed the lakeside homes and their inhabitants. The population around the lake had experienced a resurgence of growth in recent years. A strong economy, low interest rates, and the desire for more quality time brought people here with their dreams and plans for a better life. Where there was once an abundance of wooded lakefront land, people had replaced it with a dizzying array of architectural styles, buildings, and curious lakefront amenities. It made for great sightseeing, and they rode through the waterfront exhibit while making their way around the lake, each stop on the tour providing its own unique experience.

They passed several homes and came to stop at a beautiful old home up on the hillside. The estate stood as a testament to a time and an architectural style long since past. At this particular spot, rising up from the riprap shoreline above the neatly manicured and freshly watered lawn, stood a hand-laid stone mansion unlike the mostly frame homes that surrounded the lake. There were two full floors of what they imagined to be endless rooms, most of which looked out onto the lake. Topped with blue and gray slate and framed with copper, the home was arguably one of the finest on the lakeshore. They could imagine the earliest occupants, strolling across the lawn in Sunday suits and sundresses, with parasols resting on women's shoulders and twirling behind their heads. On this day, they saw a young couple lounging on a hammock strung between two trees, while their shirtless young boys played catch on the lawn beside them. As they observed, Rick shared with his guests what he knew of the one hundred and twenty-year history of the home. Having heard his explanation many times before, his wife and daughter trailed off into their own thoughts.

They continued their cruise around the lake, each house eliciting a different set of comments. Rick did not notice at first, but Carol had gotten up and moved to the front of the boat with the children. It was not until she spoke that he saw her standing there.

"Rick, I think you need to turn around," she said.

She was standing at the bow, and his daughter Caitlin was standing right beside her. He was facing forward, keeping an eye on the boat traffic in front of him. They were both looking toward the back of the boat, off toward his left.

"What's the matter?" he asked.

"Dad, there's something in the water back there," Caitlin yelled, a concerned look on her face.

"Have a seat, and we'll take a look," he said.

Without hesitation, he spun the wheel and gradually accelerated. The boat banked left and hit an oncoming wave. He completed the turn, straightened the wheel, and pushed down hard on the throttle. The boat, although weighted down with a full load, rose to plane quickly. It sped forward, and he looked to Carol and Caitlin for direction.

"Right over there," Carol shouted. She stretched out her arm and pointed off the right side of the boat.

He followed her direction to a spot in the water some fifty yards from where they were. There was something in the water, all right, but he could not make out what it was. He was not sure if the feeling came from the girls in front, maybe from the looks on their faces or the tone of their voices, but he felt an unnerving sensation. Something was terribly wrong.

Rick looked again at the lifeless face. It was the face of a young man, probably sixteen or seventeen years old. His long brown hair was matted down, and there were scattered pieces of seaweed intermingled with it. The color of his skin was unlike anything Rick had ever seen before. The finest special effects and make-up artists cannot recreate this particular color, as it is possible only in death. His eyelids were closed lightly like those of a sleeping child. His nostrils made no movement, and there was no sound of breathing. His cold, blue lips pressed together, and no seam was visible where they met. A trickle of blood stained the corner of his mouth, a blazing contrast to the dull bluish background, and Rick noticed a small puncture wound just under his chin.

He grabbed the young man by the shoulder strap of his life vest and spun him around. Then Rick looked over his shoulder for the boat. It was there, some ten or twelve feet away. He began to swim, stretching out his free arm and following it with a strong scissor-kick. He pulled the young man behind, and the water crested over the youth's forehead and his face. It streamed over his nostrils and closed lips, but he simply lay there, peaceful and unaware. With five or six strokes, they made it to the boat, and Rick grasped frantically for the swim ladder that Tom had lowered. He grabbed the ladder and pulled himself close, and the young man followed.

At most, thirty seconds had passed, but it seemed they were in the water much longer. Rick had difficulty catching his breath as the excitement knocked the wind out of him like a ferocious blow to the stomach. He gasped for air but could take none in. His eyes were wide, and he searched his brain for some direction. None came.

Rick heard Tom yelling at him. He looked up to see Tom kneeling on the rear swim deck, looking down on both of them.

"Rick, you have to give him CPR. He's not breathing," Tom said.

Rick was not sure how Tom knew the young man was not breathing, but it was a good guess. The opportunity to check his pulse never presented itself, since Rick's focus was to get them both back to the boat, and to land, as quickly as possible.

"Rick, he's not breathing. You have to give him CPR," Tom repeated.

"I . . . I . . ." was all he could get out as he struggled for air.

He looked at Tom, unable to speak. What Rick really wanted to say was, *"You get into the water and give him CPR yourself if that's what you think he needs,"* but instead he just kept looking up at the swim deck. Tom could tell he was having trouble breathing, and he reached down and grabbed hold of Rick under the arm.

Rick's hand was wrapped tight around the young man's vest. In his haste, Rick had entered the water with no vest or flotation device of his own. Tom held on to Rick as he kicked furiously to keep himself afloat. His heart pumped wildly, and his lungs felt somewhat regenerated from the moist, sweet air coming off the water. He pressed two fingers firmly to the side of the young man's neck, just under the jaw line. He tried to hold it there for a few seconds but did not feel anything. He moved his fingers around a bit, seeking the groove where the artery rests neatly between neck muscles and just under the skin. He pressed firmly again and once more felt nothing.

The thought of giving CPR came and went. He and the young man bobbed around in the water, and the waves hit them, sometimes hard. While he'd been required to perform a similar CPR maneuver for a lifesaving class some twenty years ago, current conditions would not allow for it. He tried to think if there was any possible way of getting the young man up on the swim deck, and that thought passed as well. His strength was near gone, his body running on the remaining adrenaline surging through his veins. Tom would be of no help. Rick looked again at the young man, their faces just inches apart. He removed his fingers from the man's neck and with an open hand, slapped him on the cheek. He slapped him repeatedly before realizing it would not help. Rick laid his hand gently on the youth's cheek and said to him, "C'mon, breathe. You have to breathe!"

The young man just lay there on his back, and Rick looked over his profile. He focused on the trickle of blood that dripped from the corner of the young man's mouth. The blood had dried, yet the surface of it still glistened with lake water. He said again, "Please, for God's sake, breathe."

He looked up at Tom and in his eyes saw the fear that this young man was dead. Rick knew Tom must be seeing the look of defeat in his own eyes, and they said nothing.

Just then, Rick heard a slight sound from the young man. In a single instant, the young man's chest thrust upward, and a stream of water, mucous, and blood escaped from his lips and flowed down each side of his mouth. A short gasp followed, and a rapid succession of coughs, each one emptying a portion of the contents accumulated in his lungs. The coughing seemed endless, but eventually it stopped, and the young man opened his eyes.

"My God, he's alive," Rick said to Tom.

He had not noticed, but Carol and Linda were looking over the side of the boat. In the front of the boat, the kids were watching as well.

"He's alive. He's alive," Rick yelled.

They had planned to take the kids tubing, and they had an inflated tube tied down to the rear engine hatch. Rick yelled up to Linda to untie it and drop it in the water.

Rick, Linda, and Caitlin had made a trip to the marina earlier in the morning before their guests arrived, interested in getting a new, larger tube that would accommodate more than one person. Caitlin was tired of riding alone and wanted one large enough for at least one person to join her. They had decided on a blue-green three-person raft, which resembled a full-size inflatable mattress. Someone must have been looking out for them that day, because their circular doughnut tube would have been no help now. Linda lowered it into the water and tied it off on one of the rear cleats.

They struggled, but with some assistance from their revived friend, Tom and Rick were able to get the young man up on the raft. Rick crawled up onto the raft with him, and he learned that the young man's name was Brian. Rick looked into Brian's eyes, and they appeared glazed but responsive. Brian seemed to understand and could communicate, and Rick felt a slight sense of relief. He asked if Brian could move his feet and looked down to see them moving back and forth. He asked the same about Brian's hands and fingers, and Brian raised them, arms and all, to show him they still worked. Rick asked him if anything hurt or was bothering him, and Brian told him only his chin hurt. Rick concluded he must have fallen, struck his chin on the jet ski's handlebar, and knocked himself out. There was a bruise the size of a small apple around the puncture wound under his chin, and it would surely remain sore for many days.

Rick rolled back into the water, climbed the swim ladder, and Tom helped him into the boat. He hurried to the wheel, started the engine, and forcefully thrust the throttle down. The boat lurched forward, and everyone grasped desperately for something to hold. He looked back to see Tom holding the line to the raft.

"Take it easy, Rick. We don't want to lose him," Tom said.

Rick figured they were about thirty yards from shore, and he headed for the closest dock. There was a man and a woman on the dock, and he noted a look of concern on their faces.

"We have an injured man on board," Rick yelled to them. "Call 9-1-1, and tell them we need paramedics and an ambulance."

The woman took off back to shore and ambled up the hill and into her house.

"Would you mind if we dock here until help arrives?" Rick asked.

"By all means," the man said.

He made it to the dock, swung the back end of the boat around so he could approach parallel to it, and cut the engine. The man reached for a line from Caitlin and quickly helped to tie up the front of the boat. Rick hopped off the back, grabbed a line from Linda, and secured the stern.

"Thanks for your help," Rick said to the man.

"I watched everything that happened out there, and I think you just saved that man's life," the man said.

"I'll feel much better once the paramedics get here," Rick replied.

The minutes passed like hours, but eventually the paramedics arrived, and they ran down the dock. There were two of them: a man and a woman. The man carried a large chest and a backboard, and the woman had another large handled chest. Close behind were two police officers, and they appeared uneasy in their hurried run down to the dock.

Brian was still lying on the raft next to the dock, floating, and appearing peaceful. He looked up at an unrecognizable point in the sky and seemed to analyze it with blind eyes and a protected mind. They hoisted him up onto the dock, raft and all, and the paramedics immediately attended to him. As they worked, they asked questions, and Rick provided answers. The rest of the party remained on the boat, shocked and silenced.

The paramedics' main concern was the amount of time Brian was "down." They were trying to assess how long he had been face down in the water, not breathing, and how long until he was revived. Rick estimated it took thirty seconds to turn the boat around and get to him. It was maybe another minute until he started breathing again. He could not be sure, though, and had no idea how long Brian was face down in the water before Carol and Caitlin noticed him.

All eyes watched, from the boat and from the spectators gathering on the shore, as the paramedics worked. Rick could hear Brian responding to their questions. He seemed lucid and responsive, but he was not moving. They had strapped him to the backboard and had his head immobilized with Velcro straps and a foam collar around his neck.

As quickly as they arrived, the paramedics and the police officers left, and Rick found himself standing alone on the dock. His heart was still beating fast, and he felt chilled as he stood there, soaking wet and wearing only his swimming trunks. His pulse pounded in his temples.

The sound of the car horn from behind startled him. He straightened in his seat and through reflex, hit the gas. There was an opening of at least six car lengths, and he hurried to close the gap.

He was daydreaming again.

Rick tried to shake the thoughts in his mind, and the visions they had conjured up. It was over two years now since that day on the lake, yet every minute detail of that event remained fresh in his memory. Often while sitting in the car on his way to or from work, the memory would return, and he would transport himself back to that time and place.

Lately, he had been thinking a lot about that day, while not altogether sure why. He did know that as he replayed the events of that day, of his encounter with that young man, he found certain points in the chronology where emotion overcame him. He replayed his entry into the water and criticized his lack of judgment. Although he was a trained lifeguard, he had entered the water with no lifesaving gear or flotation device. *Stupid.* Things could have played out much differently. He could have ended up on the bottom of that lake, he thought. He could see the blue-gray death mask of the young man and wondered if he really was dead, and if so, for how long. He played back the thoughts that had been in his mind as he floated in the water with him, looking at the youth's cold and lifeless face and praying, hoping for him to breathe again. How did he start to breathe again? What bothered Rick the most was not knowing what happened to the young man afterward. Did he recover? Was he lying in a long-term care facility somewhere with irreparable brain damage? Did they get to him in time? Those thoughts created knots in his stomach and sometimes brought tears to his eyes.

He focused his attention back on the road and his journey home after another long day at the office. He checked his watch and noted that while he had been in the car for almost an hour already, he was not quite halfway home. One of these days, he would get some sense and find work that was closer to where he lived. The two-hour congested road trips grated on his patience.

The weather was not unlike that day on the lake, he thought. The sky was bright and cloudless, the heat intense, and the humidity normal for a Midwest summer day. He could tolerate this kind of weather in shorts and a t-shirt, but with long sleeves and a tie, albeit loosened around his neck, he was quite uncomfortable. He turned the air conditioning up to its highest level, and it bled over the music coming from the radio. It could not keep up with the sweltering heat, and his back stuck to his shirt, which stuck to the back of the seat. He could tell it was hot out when sweat dripped down his calves, and today, the top edges of his socks were damp.

Cars packed the expressway, like most days. As he looked through the windshield, the heat that radiated from the engine under the hood distorted his vision, rising up through the metal like a wavy-clear ghost escaping its grave. The black, leather-like dashboard absorbed the heat of the day, and he knew that if he touched it, it would burn him.

The pain of an earlier headache returned, and he felt a dull throb that started in his temples and pierced through to the backs of his eyes. He fished through the glove box, pushing aside the bottle of antacid tablets to get to the aspirin. With one hand, he flipped the cap off and into his lap, and steered with his knee while pouring two tablets into the other hand. There was nothing to drink, so he pressed his tongue against the roof of his mouth to create some saliva. He tilted his head back, opened his mouth wide, tossed the tablets to the back of his throat, and swallowed. He knew relief would not come quickly.

His cell phone rang, and he groped in his right front pocket for it. He flipped it open and noticed from the caller ID that it was his wife.

"Hi honey, what's up?"

"Rick, where are you," Linda said in a hurried voice.

"I'm on the expressway, probably another hour away," he said.

Before he could finish his sentence, she said, "You have to get home right away. Caitlin's been hurt."

"What happened?"

"She was hit by a car coming home from school," she said, agitated and struggling with her words. "I got a call from the school. They told me they rushed her to the emergency room. I'm here now, and it's not good."

It's not good.

"Oh, here comes the doctor," she said. "I need to run. Get here as soon as you can—Hillside Memorial," she added and hung up before he could say anything further.

He turned off his phone and set it on the seat next to him. Beads of sweat dripped down his forehead. He felt as if he was in an oven and someone just turned the dial up to broil. His shirt collapsed around him and stuck to his skin.

He was completely alone.

He reached for the knob and turned off the radio. At the same time, his foot hit the accelerator. He had to react quickly with a sharp right turn to keep from hitting the car in front of him. Traffic filled all the lanes and cars lined up for miles on a short-course to nowhere. He veered off into the rightmost lane, which drivers of broken down or emergency vehicles used. He categorized his own car as an emergency vehicle and sped on, covering more ground in thirty seconds than he did in the last twenty minutes and forgetting to notice the seventy-five mile-per-hour speed he had reached. He came to a junction of on-and-off ramps and stayed the course for fear that the street traffic would be even worse. Unknowingly, he braked lightly and proceeded through the junction. Once through, he hit the gas hard and continued up the shoulder.

Behind him, somewhere in the distance, a siren erupted and grew louder with each passing second. The siren could not compete with the machine-gun-like sound his car made as he sped past the slight gaps in the cars of the frozen motorists. Eventually though, the siren was so loud it was all he could hear, and he looked in the rearview mirror to find a bar of blue-white-blue-white flashing lights, moving in perfect synchronization to the music of the siren.

I can't afford to stop. I have to get to the hospital. If I can just ride the shoulder a bit longer, I can get off at the next exit and start across town.

The bright openness of the shoulder ahead of him began to dim and shrink as he approached a vehicle with a flat tire. The lane to the left was full of cars and to the right of the stopped vehicle was a steep bank, not manageable by even the best of off-road vehicles. There was no option but to brake, hard and fast. The brakes locked for an instant; then the anti-lock feature engaged and brought the car to a more controlled, yet still sudden, stop.

"Rick, I think you need to turn around," he thought he heard someone say, but there was no one around to tell him that. He stared blankly through the windshield. His temples ached and his vision blurred. Instantly, the expressway became an expanse of open water. In his vision, he saw something floating in front of him. He strained to see, and soon he realized what he was looking at. It was Caitlin, face down in the water. He didn't know how long she had been there, and he couldn't get any closer to help her. He couldn't get any closer.

"Sir, step out of the car, slowly and with your hands above your head," Rick heard from the police car's loudspeaker. He shook his head to clear the vision.

He unbuckled the seatbelt with one hand as he reached for the door handle. He got out, turned to face the rear of his car, and in haste, began to approach the patrol car.

"Sir, stop and stay right where you are," the police officer shouted through the loudspeaker. Rick heard him and stopped, standing at the side of the road, flustered and sweating, with his arms raised straight above his head. He was a spectacle for the gawking of the car-parked audience. He was sure they were thinking he was some type of criminal, but that was the least of his concerns.

The police officer got out of his vehicle and stretched to his full size. He was quite large, in both height and girth, and if other people were not around, Rick would be worried. The police officer had a chiseled face, and his eyes hid behind a pair of gold-rimmed Ray Ban aviators. Rick noticed that his right hand firmly rested on his gun, and he was approaching with a long stride. He did not get too close, but came to a stop some three feet from Rick.

"Officer, my daughter—" Rick said.

"Sir, keep your hands up and slowly turn around," the officer shouted.

With a swift move, he came up behind Rick, grabbed Rick's right hand, and forcefully brought it down and behind him. The cop's left hand firmly grabbed Rick's left arm and kept it close to his body. He completed the maneuver by turning Rick slightly and pushing him against the back of the car, face down. A quick interrogation ensued, most questions focusing on Rick's irrational behavior and his need to ride the shoulder at excessive speeds. The questions seemed more like allegations, as Rick did not have the opportunity to speak. Being quiet for the time being was probably a good idea. The police officer finally asked Rick to explain himself and paused to let him respond.

Rick tried to relax so that when he did speak he would be able to say something coherent and convincing, but that proved difficult.

"Officer, my daughter has been in a terrible accident, and I need to get to the hospital."

The police officer looked straight at him for just a moment. Then, without saying anything, he lifted Rick up off the car and walked him back to his vehicle. He opened the rear door, nudged Rick in, and closed the door. The police officer got in the front seat.

"What is your daughter's name, and what hospital is she at?" he asked.

Rick told him. The police officer grabbed the microphone attached to his left front shoulder and spoke into it. He shared the information with a woman at the other end and waited for a reply. After a long time, the radio speaker came to life, and the woman confirmed what he had told her. Rick listened to the woman's voice, and detected something unsettling in the way she spoke.

"I'm probably not supposed to do this, but I'm going to drive you to the hospital," the officer said. "I'll call for a tow truck to come and get your vehicle, and you can pick it up later."

The police officer started the engine, put it into gear, and sped away with aggression in his acceleration. The flashing lights continued to strobe from the earlier pursuit. He reached to the dashboard and flipped a switch, and the car's siren came to life. Cars parted desperately in their congested mess, allowing the squad car to maneuver left around Rick's car and the flat tire, then the squad car sped up the shoulder. At the next off-ramp, the officer exited and headed across town to the hospital. The streets opened themselves up to the roaring and flashing signals, and Rick's new friend made his own attempt at sea parting. In what would have taken Rick at least thirty minutes, the police officer made it there in ten, and he brought Rick directly to the emergency room entrance.

Rick thanked him and hurried from the squad car. The emergency room doors parted as he approached, and he hurried to the reception desk just inside. Before she could ask, he told the young receptionist his name and that he was here to see his daughter, Caitlin Bradley. It seemed she had difficulty looking at him. Her gaze darted up, then back down to something in front of her on the desk.

"Your daughter is in room 4-B, just behind me on the left," she said in a hushed, nervous tone. He quickly stepped around her desk and ran down the hall.

He got to Caitlin's room and went in. Inside the room was a single bed, where she lay quiet and motionless. Linda sat in a chair at the bedside, and he could tell she had been crying. He looked back at his daughter and looked for clues that would tell him something about her condition. There was a gauze bandage wrapped around her head, it seemed just lightly, and her hair neatly draped over it. Her face looked like an angel's face, rosy-pink and flawless. There was a small plastic tube coming from her mouth, and he traced it to a large piece of equipment off to the right, which was pumping and hissing and beeping. The bed sheet was up to her neck, and he saw only a mummy-form of her from the neck down.

Linda stood up and came to him. He kissed her gently on the forehead and hugged her, holding her tight and trying to comfort her as she began to cry again. He held her for a long time as he stared at Caitlin, seeing her but not knowing if she really was there. He relaxed his embrace and leaned back to look at Linda.

"How is she, and what happened?" he asked. He waited while Linda wiped her moist red eyes and took a few deep breaths, making a brave attempt to compose herself.

"I received a call from the school nurse about two hours ago. She said a car in front of the gymnasium had hit Caitlin. Someone called an ambulance immediately, but when it arrived, the paramedics found Caitlin unresponsive and not breathing. They resuscitated her and transported her here. The doctor came by and explained her condition. That's when I called you. She has a broken leg, but that's the least of his concerns. The paramedics and police on the scene said the car hit her left side, and she flew quite a distance. She appears to have excessive trauma to the head. The doctor thinks she struck her head on the pavement when she landed. There's no real visible damage, except for a small scrape above her ear."

She paused to catch her breath.

"They're not sure of the cause, but she did stop breathing, and by all accounts it was for at least five minutes. The paramedics got her breathing again, but they had to continue CPR while bringing her here because her heart wouldn't keep beating on its own. It still won't. They put her on a ventilator to keep her breathing. They're running tests on her brain and heart, and they're not sure of the damage. Rick, they're not sure she's going to make it," and with those words, she began to weep.

"She's a strong and healthy young girl," he said as he tried to reassure her. "She's going to be fine." But his words were weak, and he knew it. He took Linda by the arm and led her back to her chair. He grabbed another chair from against the wall and pulled it up so he could sit next to her. He reached over, grabbed her hand, and held it tight. They sat there, together but alone with their thoughts.

The door opened and slammed against the wall, startling them. A nurse walked into the room and stood at the foot of the bed, lifting the chart from its holster and reviewing it. She was a middle-aged black woman wearing a simple print top, white pants, and white nurses' shoes. She looked fit, and her skin was medium brown and flawless. Her jet-black hair was cropped close to her skull. She had delicate facial features and was strikingly beautiful.

"I'm really sorry," she said. "I've asked Maintenance a dozen times to fix that door so it doesn't swing open like that. I hope I didn't startle you."

"No. It's okay," Rick said.

She smiled at him and knew he was lying. She looked to Linda, acknowledging her, then returned her attention to the chart.

"My name is Tanya, and I'll be taking care of your Caitlin. I was here when the paramedics brought her in. Her left leg is broken in three places. We've stabilized it for now, and we'll talk about how we're going to address the leg when the orthopedic surgeon comes by later. We've run a battery of tests to assess brain and heart function, and the doctor will be back shortly to go over the results with you. For now, we will keep her on the ventilator and do everything we can to make her comfortable. Can I get you anything?"

Rick looked at Linda. She looked at him, and they both shook their heads. The nurse straightened the sheets, walked over to the ventilator, made a few adjustments, and scrawled some notes on the chart. She walked to the foot of the bed and returned the chart to its holster.

"If you need anything, just press that red button," she said, pointing to a wired nurse-call button hanging from the side of the bed. "I'll be checking in periodically, and the doctor should be by within the hour." Then she was gone. As they turned to say goodbye, all they saw was the door closing behind her.

"She seems nice," Linda said.

"Yeah."

The next hour and a half was torturous. They spoke little and instead kept their gazes on Caitlin. They watched her face, her eyes, her nostrils, and her chest, searching for any indication that she was in there, behind those eyes, beyond that mask. There was nothing. It was hard for them not to think the worst, but they were both running through worst-case scenarios in their minds. They certainly were not ready to lose their only child, yet they seemed to have no control over what was happening.

It was not an hour, like the nurse had said, but they were glad when the doctor finally walked in.

"Hello, Mr. and Mrs. Bradley," the doctor said. He turned to

Rick. "You must be Caitlin's father. Mr. Bradley, I'm Dr. Robinson."

"Hello, Doctor," Rick replied, as he extended a hand. The doctor took Rick's hand in both of his own and gave it a firm yet friendly squeeze.

"Mrs. Bradley," he said as he turned to Linda and shook her hand with the same two-hand grip. "I was able to assess Caitlin's condition when she first came to the emergency room. Since she was unconscious and not breathing for several minutes, I was concerned about brain function and possible damage. She was unresponsive to all external tests, so I ordered a CAT scan and a number of other tests. I also ran an EKG and a heart scan to rule out any heart irregularities or damage."

"And what did you find," Rick blurted out, interrupting him.

"Her heart is fine. We found nothing that could have caused her heart to stop beating after the accident, and there is no heart damage. She has the perfect heart of a healthy teenage girl."

"But . . ." Rick continued for him. He knew there was a "but" coming from the doctor's presentation and the tone of his voice.

"However, we did not get the positive results we were looking for from the tests on her brain. We're not finding any brain activity, and that is our primary concern."

You think? It was all that ran through Rick's head, and he immediately felt bad about the sarcasm he was feeling. Somehow, Rick thought the doctor noticed it.

"Mr. and Mrs. Bradley, Caitlin has experienced a serious trauma to the head. We are going to move her to the ICU so that we can monitor her situation closely. The brain is quite remarkable and has the ability to heal itself over time. We really need to let her rest and give her body and her brain a chance to recover from the shock to her system."

Linda spoke up. "Doctor, do you think she'll pull through this?" The words came out one at a time, interspersed with quick breaths. She was having difficulty controlling her sobbing.

"All we can do right now is let her rest." He reached out and put a hand on Linda's crossed arms, trying to reassure her. She lowered her head and continued to cry. A large tear dropped from her eye and landed on his hand. "She needs you to be strong for her." He removed his hand, nodded to Rick, and walked to the door. He turned back as he reached it. "I'll check back in with you in a couple of hours," was all he said, and he walked out of the room.

Before they could say anything, the door flew open again, and Tanya walked in with two orderlies trailing close behind.

"We're going to take her up to ICU, which is on the eighth floor. Why don't you come up with us?" Tanya said.

"What about the ventilator?" Rick asked.

"It has a battery backup that allows it to run for about sixty minutes on its own. We'll have her up to her room in five."

Rick and Linda spent that evening and most of the next two days sitting by their daughter's bedside. She had visitors throughout the day, which helped to keep them optimistic; they had to be. Friends and family took turns for short visits, and in the late afternoons, her friends from school came by. While saddened, everyone tried to act cheerfully. They touched her and spoke to her and left cards, flowers, and stuffed animals.

Linda and Rick had no one to go home to. They stayed the evenings with Caitlin in her room, stretched out on reclining chairs. Tanya had done her best to make them comfortable, and surprisingly, she always seemed to be around. On the evening of their third day there, Tanya came into the room to check on Caitlin. It was late, maybe ten-thirty, and Linda was asleep beside Rick. Sleep would not come easily for Rick that evening.

"Tanya, do you ever go home?" Rick asked.

"Sure," she replied but said nothing more.

Rick looked at her, and she returned his inquisitive stare. She knew he wanted more, but she declined temporarily. She checked Caitlin's IV and adjusted the drip rate. She continued with her scripted regimen of adjusting the sheets and making sure the room was in order. She pulled the chart from the bed, reviewed it briefly, and made a few notations.

"I've been taking on a couple of extra shifts," Tanya offered after a minute. "I'm covering for a sick friend, and I can use the extra money." She continued to look at the chart. "When you two are sleeping, I run home, feed the cat, and get some sleep. I'm usually back here before breakfast."

It sounded plausible, but at the same time, Rick had the feeling she was holding something back. He would not get anything more from her that evening.

To Rick, Tanya was a fantastic nurse and seemed to genuinely care for Caitlin. She really did seem to be around all the time, certainly more than one would expect. In addition, she was always trying to make Caitlin comfortable, giving her short massages, adjusting her pillows, and brushing her hair back from her face. Each time before she left, she would put a hand to Caitlin's face and look at her for just a few seconds.

Rick tossed and turned that evening as sleep escaped him. He typically had trouble sleeping when something was on his mind—if he had a tangled project at work or if he and Linda were helping Caitlin work through the latest teenage crisis. Tonight, it was all Caitlin, and thoughts of her bombarded him. He began to replay their lives together, rewinding to the many happy episodes the three of them shared. In time, he found himself crying, overcome with emotion. Caitlin was a fantastic young woman, and he and Linda were fortunate to have a very close and loving relationship with her. They were great friends, best friends, and in spite of what her teenage friends thought, Caitlin still believed her parents knew everything and could do no wrong.

He was not willing to let their relationship end.

That night, his memory of the day on the lake returned. As he had done many times, he relived the sequence of events as though it had happened the day before. He thought about how the young man started to breathe again and how it made him feel. Somehow, Rick felt he had the ability to save the young man's life. How he wished he could save his own daughter.

Did I use up my one chance? Rick thought. Tears streamed down his face, and he was overwhelmed with guilt and remorse.

He must have dozed off, because he was startled awake by the slamming of the door against the wall. Sleep clouded his mind as he searched the darkened room. There was no sound except for the breathing of the ventilator and its corresponding heartbeat. He looked toward the door and watched as it closed by itself. Linda was at his side sleeping peacefully, and he heard slight wisps of air coming from her nostrils. It was dark, and he could see only her outline. He put his hand on her arm and felt her breathing. Then he heard a cough. When his brain did not register any corresponding movement from his wife's arm, he knew it was not his wife who coughed. He heard the cough again, and then he saw Caitlin in the shadows, stirring in her bed and pushing up coughs through the ventilator tube.

"Linda, wake up. It's Caitlin. She's back. She's breathing on her own!"

He reached for the nurse-call button and pressed it hard and repeatedly as he got up from his chair to look her over.

"Take it easy, baby, the nurse is on her way," he reassured her.

The room door swung open fast and slammed against the wall. Two nurses ran in and were at Caitlin's bedside in seconds. Before the door could swing closed, Dr. Robinson strode in.

"I just happened to be on the floor starting my evening rounds when the room alarms went off. Let's see what we have here."

One nurse had instructed Caitlin to give her three strong coughs, and she removed the tube from Caitlin's throat with one swift motion. The nurses moved away, allowing the doctor to step up to the bed.

"Mom, Dad," they heard Caitlin say in a hushed, almost silent voice. Rick and Linda were overcome with emotion. Linda leaned over, hugged her daughter close, and cried tears of joy.

"I'd say we just witnessed a miracle," Dr. Robinson said.

"Where's Tanya," Rick asked. "She would want to know that Caitlin's back with us."

"She just ended her shift," one of the nurses said.

Rick headed for the door and opened it. He scanned the hallway, hoping Tanya might still be around. He looked down the corridor to the left and to the right, but saw no one. The nurses' station was right across from him, and he saw three other nurses, all glued to their computer screens. Beyond the station was a short hallway with an elevator at the far end. Someone was just getting on.

"Tanya! Tanya! It's Caitlin. She's back!"

He stared at the person getting on the elevator, who had stopped upon hearing his shouts. The person stepped back and turned around.

"Tanya!" he shouted again.

He looked at her, and she looked at him.

It was you, he thought.

Her mouth formed a huge smile, and a tear dripped down her cheek. She turned and got on the elevator, and the doors came together quietly behind her.

Notes on
The Pass

In the summer of 2003, in the month of July to be exact, some greater power called upon my family to partake in a unique twist of fate. We were steered to a particular time, to a particular place, to serve a specific function. The strings of a master puppeteer were in full motion. On that particular summer day, unbeknownst to us, we had but one purpose: to save a young man's life.

My wife and I and our two children were up at our condominium on Lake Delavan for the weekend, and our good friends came up with their two boys to spend the weekend with us. After their arrival, it wasn't long before we were on the lake, in our boat and cruising the shoreline on our way to find that perfect place to drop the tube into the water. The kids were excited and anxious, sitting in the bow of the boat and wondering when we were going to stop the boat and start the tube rides.

I am not sure why we drove around the lake the way we did on that particular day. The condominium was located on the outlet of Delavan Lake, and it was a short, slow ride to make our way through the shallow outlet. Once we made it to the main body of the lake, we could have put the tube in right there and started the rides. Instead, we kept driving, taking a scenic tour of the lake as we proceeded west along the north shore.

As we reached the western-most part of the lake, my daughter noticed something in the water behind us and brought it to my attention. As I turned the boat around to see what it was, I realized it was a person floating in the water alongside a very empty jet ski. I could see it was a young man, face down in the water, and I knew we had to get to him quickly.

We never could have imagined the events that played out over the next sixty minutes. Life played in fast-forward, but it felt like a dream. How or why certain things happened, I could not explain, but we rescued the young man and then he disappeared.

After the ambulance drove away, I found myself standing on someone's boat dock. I was alone, wet, and shivering—not because it was cold but because I think I was in shock. That shock would stay with me for most of the day and not even a substantial amount of gin could make it go away. I realized that the day's events would stay with me for the rest of my life.

In the following years, I frequently thought about what happened that day on the lake. I thought about the simple fact that the boy was lucky, that *I was lucky*, and I couldn't help but think we were all part of some grand scheme that day. That situation ended well, but the events could have played out much differently. Particular aspects of those events bothered me, and I thought about them often. Most frustrating, I wondered about the young man and if he was all right. The friends that were with us had contacted the local hospital and were told that the young man was airlifted to another facility.

That was it. That was all we knew. The more I thought back on it, the more the details of the event returned until I could play back, in my mind, every second in stunningly clear detail.

As I started my writing career in 2007, I thought that many elements of what happened that day would make a good story, so in September of that year, I penned *The Pass*. The story is partly autobiographical and historical, and includes much more detail about what actually happened on that fateful day. While I changed the names and maybe added a little color, I tried to accurately recount how I saw that day unfold and what it really meant to me—meant to all of us who were there. The second half of the story is purely fictional.

As I set out to write the story, I realized we were fortunate to have been in the right place at the right time. We were fortunate to have played a role in some cosmic reality play. Then I started to wonder: *do we only get one chance to help someone else? What if I needed to help someone again, especially someone close to me? Would I be lost, having used up my one and only chance?* I explored this idea, and it directed me as I completed the story, and in doing so, I found the answers.

I realize now that often we are simply victims of circumstance. Other times we are lead characters in a fateful play. Whatever the situation, we have to believe in the good intentions in all people and know that in a time of need, someone will be there to lend a helping hand.

I know I believe.

No Turning Back

Tommy Sanders sat motionless, not exactly sure how to deal with the situation confronting him. The roar of the airplane engines, the smell of sweat and gasoline, and the turbulence of the flight was more than he could handle. How did he get himself into this predicament, and why was he on a plane heading to a foreign country to fight a war he really didn't understand?

When he met with the U.S. Army recruiter, everything seemed pretty clear to Tommy. Sergeant Maxwell had laid it all out for him.

"Congratulations, son," Sergeant Maxwell had started. "You'll be joining the strongest and most dominant armed forces in the world. After eight weeks of basic training, you'll feel better and stronger than you've ever felt in your life. In time, you'll learn a valuable trade, make a decent salary, and earn credit toward your college education. Most important of all, you'll be able to see and experience the world."

That sounded pretty good to Tommy. Having just graduated from high school with no particular career aspirations, he felt the Army was the perfect solution for him. He would make new friends, work hard at his new job and career, and get out of the sleepy town that had been his whole world for the last eighteen years.

But at that moment, dressed in battle fatigues with a rifle resting uncomfortably across his lap and jammed in a transport plane with forty-nine of his new friends, Tommy wished he were back in that sleepy town. He wished he were back in his bedroom with his headphones on and his mother pounding on the locked bedroom door, telling him to come down for dinner. He would welcome the slap on the back of the head his drunk, no-good excuse for a father would give him when he came home from work. He would give everything he had to not be on that damn plane.

Over the plane's loudspeaker came the first words heard from anyone since they left the airfield some four hours ago.

"O.K. men, this is Captain Tracy. We'll be arriving at our destination in forty minutes. Take the time right now to be sure all of your equipment is in order and that your rifle is loaded and locked. Turn to your right and make sure your neighbor is ready to go as well. The next instructions you'll get will be at the three-minute mark as we're entering our drop zone."

Tommy turned to John Marks and said, "I don't know about you, John, but I'm not sure I'm ready for this."

"You'll be fine," John replied. "Just try to focus on our mission for today, and everything else will take care of itself. All of our training has prepared us for this. Now we just have to go out and do our jobs."

"Easy for you to say. You've been doing this Army stuff two years longer than I have. You've gone into hostile territory before. You've even shot somebody. I'm just not sure I'll be able to handle this."

"You'll be fine. Just stick close, and I'll cover your back," John said. That reassurance made Tommy feel a little better. John was a Specialist and the acting squad leader, but he was also Tommy's closest friend. Having John around made most tough times a bit easier to handle.

The next forty minutes were going to pass in a blur, Tommy thought. It just wasn't enough time to get ready, mentally or physically. In forty minutes, he'd be jumping out of an airplane with a parachute on his back and drop into an area known to be swarming with hostile rebel forces. When he hit the ground, he'd be expected to meet up with his platoon and take control of a pre-defined sector. He assumed the sector was at least pre-defined to someone else, as the platoon had not been told exactly where they were going. He'd be expected to shoot the enemy and kill them, if necessary. No matter how much training you have, you're just never ready for something like that.

To make matters worse, Tommy was exhausted. After he received his orders twenty-four hours earlier, he hadn't been able to get any sleep. His mind was racing. Could he remember all the details of the mission? Would he freeze when he actually got into battle? Would he be able to shoot, or even kill, someone? Was he prepared to die for his country? All of his questions would be answered very soon, but now they tormented him and prevented him from getting any rest. He hadn't slept in over thirty hours, and if he didn't get himself killed, he'd be up for at least another twelve.

"Hey, John, do me a favor and wake me up in thirty minutes. I've got to get a little shut-eye before the drop."

"No problem, Tommy. Sweet dreams."

It didn't take long for Tommy to doze off. In a matter of minutes, he was snoring softly in his seat, upright but leaning over on John's shoulder.

As quickly as he had fallen asleep, he awoke with a jolt. He opened his eyes but couldn't see anything. The lights were out, and there seemed to be a fog spreading throughout the cabin.

The loudspeaker crackled to life. "All right folks, this is Captain Tracy again. If you haven't noticed, we've been experiencing some pretty rough turbulence for the last half-hour, and it doesn't look like it'll be getting any better. We also experienced a malfunction of our left main engine, which we had to shut down. We're thirty minutes short of our drop zone, but we're going to have to evacuate this plane. Don't worry about the smoke—we've got that under control. Everyone put on your mask before you hurt yourself. Get into formation, clip on your static line, and complete your final inspection. We'll be getting the green light in sixty seconds."

"John, what's happening?" Tommy was still half-asleep, his heart was pumping, and he felt as though he could not move. Before Tommy heard any response, John had grabbed Tommy's mask, slid it over his head, and rested it over his face.

"There's nothing to worry about, Tommy. Just breathe easy, relax, and pull yourself together."

John stood up, clipped on Tommy's static line and then his own, and he began to inspect his equipment. He glanced over at Tommy and saw that he was just sitting there, motionless.

"Damn it, Tommy, snap out of it. Stand up and make sure your rifle is secured."

Tommy's rifle lay neatly in his lap. Tommy just stared at it, not remembering exactly how to insert the ammunition clip or lock in a round. His rifle had been his best friend all during training camp—aside from John—yet right now it seemed completely alien to him.

"All right folks, this is Captain Tracy again. We'll be at our drop zone in thirty seconds, so let's get into formation—pronto!" Tommy heard Captain Tracy's voice, but something about the way he sounded made Tommy uncomfortable. As he thought about it, John grabbed him by the arm, lifted him to his feet, and yelled into his face, "God damn it, Tommy, this is for real! I need you to get your act together and start acting like a soldier. If you don't, you're going to get somebody killed!"

The loudspeaker came to life again. "Good luck, men. We're dropping in five, four, three, two, one, GO! GO! GO!"

To Tommy, the last thirty seconds passed by in slow motion yet were gone in an instant. As the four soldiers ahead of him made their exit out the side door, John was behind Tommy, pushing him forward. As he made it to the door opening, a thought raced through his head: *don't do it!* The next thing he knew, John had pushed him out the doorway.

As he flew out of the plane, he felt a tug on his parachute cord, and seconds later heard the wind catch in his unfolding parachute above him. He quickly looked down and all around. Four soldiers had jumped ahead of him, and forty-four would be exiting the plane after him. He could see the open parachutes of the soldiers that had jumped before him, but as he strained to look above, all he could see was darkness. He looked down again and tried to make sense of where they were.

He had assumed they would drop into uninhabited, rural territory within a short distance of some type of metropolitan area. This would allow them to drop in, hopefully without much notice, and regroup once they hit the ground. From there they could proceed to their destination. Now that they had to evacuate sooner, there was no telling exactly where they were going to land.

As he glided down in the open air, Tommy could tell they had not jumped from their planned altitude either. He could already see flickering lights in the distance, and his best guess put him at about one thousand feet and falling.

Unfortunately, it was also raining. The cold drops felt like shards of steel against his cheeks. His cheeks were the only area of uncovered skin, and the wind and rain made for a painful combination. The rain covered his goggles and blurred his vision, but his fatigues would do a fine job of repelling the water everywhere else, except on the inside where his pants were soaked.

The flight down happened faster than he expected. As the ground came toward him, he tried to remember the landing procedure. He hit the ground hard, tucked into position, and rolled. When the rolling stopped, he reached behind him and attempted to unhook the parachute from his harness. Before he could reach the quick-release latch, a gust of wind caught his parachute. It filled quickly, pulled Tommy to the ground, and began to drag him.

When he was still in the air, it seemed to Tommy that they were landing in an open field, but as he was being pulled across the ground, he could tell he was in a cornfield. The stubs of cornstalks remained after the harvest, and they scraped, poked, and tore at his body. All he heard was the breaking of the stubs as he crashed against them. His body twisted and turned, and he struggled to reach behind to free himself from the torture. He got his fingers on the latch and gave it a twist, and the parachute freed itself and continued its flight across the field.

Tommy remained motionless for a moment, trying to assess the damage. He wondered if anything else could possibly go wrong. His mission had not even started, yet he had already been through hell. His fatigues did a good job of preventing any puncture wounds, but his body was sore. He felt like he did after that first day of football practice after the long summer break. He got to his feet and looked around. About a hundred yards from where he stood, he saw the fluttering parachutes of other men in his platoon, and he ran to them as fast as he could.

As he ran he looked all around. Half of his platoon was still in the air, and they looked like jellyfish floating down from the sky. The other half was on the ground, scrambling to connect with their designated team. From ahead, he heard someone yell, "Sanders! Move it!" He recognized John's voice and continued running. He reached John, and before he could catch his breath and say something, John gave him an order.

"Sanders—you, Mitchell, Davis, and Kroch follow me." John had already sent the others in various directions. "Let's spread out and make our way to that shed, as fast as we can."

The shed John was talking about was approximately two hundred yards from where they stood. Heading for the shed sounded like a good idea to Tommy. It beat standing in the middle of the open field, waiting for someone to shoot them.

As they approached the shed, gunfire rang out. Tommy could see the orange flame-flickers of light from what appeared to be a thousand guns strewn across the landscape. He had watched enough westerns in his life to know this was your standard ambush, with the locals lining the perimeter of the field and his platoon like sitting ducks in the middle.

Tommy was about ten yards from the shed when he hit the dirt. Immediately, he was up on his elbows, crawling the remainder of the way. He made it to the shed and sat up with his back against the wall.

As he took a moment to catch his breath, he looked out into the field. The rest of his platoon was out there, with no cover and nowhere to go. Though they were a couple of hundred yards away, he knew exactly what they were going through. The gunfire was deafening, and the screaming coming from some of the men sickened him. His friends returned fire, their efforts appearing like nothing more than fireflies on a hot summer night. Some of the men had not yet landed. They could do nothing but hang in the air and wait for the enemy to shoot at them as though they were clay pigeons.

Tommy heard John yell, "Davis, you and Mitchell make your way over to that silo. Sanders, you and Kroch provide cover."

Tommy looked down at the rifle that was still secured in its drop bag. Why he didn't have it in his hands already, he didn't know. He pulled it out, made sure the safety was off, and raised it into the crook of his arm. As Davis and Mitchell sprinted for the silo, Tommy squeezed the trigger, but nothing happened. Kroch's gun was exploding next to him, laying ground fire as he was ordered. Tommy checked his gun again, squeezed the trigger, and again nothing happened. He looked out toward the silo where Davis and Mitchell were running and saw Davis take a round in the chest. Davis fell to the ground and lay motionless. Mitchell dove to the dirt and rolled up against the silo wall.

In a split second, John was in Tommy's face. "God damn it, Tommy. You just got Davis killed. What the hell is the matter with you!"

He grabbed Tommy by his fatigues, both hands filled with material, close under his chin. John pulled Tommy close and yelled at him again. There was disappointment, disgust, and anger on John's face. Tommy tried to speak, but couldn't. He tried to move, but couldn't. John started shaking him, banging his head against the wall of the shed. Tommy heard the words come out of John's mouth as if in slow motion, in a deep tone, and hardly recognizable. Tommy shut his eyes tight, and started screaming, "Leave me alone. I'm sorry! I'm sorry! I'm sorry!"

John gave Tommy one final shake.

Tommy opened his eyes. John was still there, staring straight at him. The look on John's face was different. What Tommy saw there now was compassion, understanding, and concern.

"Hey Tommy, it's me. C'mon, buddy, wake up. We're coming up to the drop zone."

Tommy's heart stopped. "What did you just say?" He looked around at the rest of the platoon, all of whom seemed to be looking at him.

"Take it easy, Tommy. You dozed off for a while and had a little nightmare. The captain wants us to make final preparations for departure. Check your parachute and your rifle, and be ready to go in sixty seconds."

As Tommy tried to clear his head and make sense of what just happened, beads of sweat formed on his brow. His heart was beating so fast he felt as though it might burst out of his chest. His mind kept replaying the terror of his recent experience, and the thoughts made him sick.

"All right, folks, this is Captain Tracy again. We'll be at our drop zone in thirty seconds, so let's get into formation—pronto!"

Tommy realized that what he'd experienced in his mind was only the beginning. He stood up and got into line. He looked behind him and saw his good friend John standing there. Tommy wondered, *Am I dreaming now?* He hoped that by looking at John's face he would get some further insight. John gave him a wink and nudged him toward the door. As the "go" light flashed over the doorway, he walked forward. When he made it to the door, he stuck his head out into the open air, leaned forward, and jumped.

Notes on
No Turning Back

No Turning Back is the first story I wrote after I made the decision
to leave my business career behind so I could pursue my long-held
dream of becoming a full-time writer. I made the career decision
after years of planning and much deliberation, and it was this story
that sent me on my way.

I remember the night, not too long ago, that I told my good
friend I was retiring. He looked at me, befuddled. I don't think he
was necessarily surprised at what I said, but he just had difficulty getting it to register. I know *retire* was not the right word to use, because
who retires at the age of forty-four? There were other reasons and
other forces in play, however, that made the use of the word appropriate and necessary. In reality, I was simply moving on to my next
career, and while I was certainly retiring the suits and storing away
the business shingle, I had no plans to move to Florida and play
shuffleboard for the rest of my years. I had a plan and an objective to
accomplish. I had stories to write.

It was a good twenty-five years ago that I first had the crazy idea
of becoming a writer. I knew from the start that there would be no
way to juggle writing, my professional career, and my responsibility
to, and desire to be with, my family. I also knew I did not want to

wait until I actually hit retirement age before I started writing. Official retirement age was an eternity away, and who knew if I would even make it or have any ability to write when that time actually arrived. I had to try something different.

I had prepared a plan, and with that plan, I set my bearings. I put everything on the line, and with a bit of luck, endless support from my family, and the outrageous goal of jamming thirty years of work into fifteen, I was off and on my way. Somehow, the plan worked and the rest, as they say, is history. There was no turning back.

The idea for *No Turning Back* came from the endless news reports on our country's involvement in the Iraq war. At the time, we were three years into the war, and it seemed not a day passed that there was not at least one war-related story in the news. I heard a story about a helicopter mission, and my first thought hit me hard. *What must be going through the minds of the young men and women on that helicopter?* I could only imagine, but I needed to know. I needed to understand.

I put myself on a transport plane with a young man by the name of Tommy Sanders, a proud American who we can all relate to and whose only objective was to serve his country. I went along for the ride in an effort to find out what was on Tommy's mind, and through the course of the story, he told me.

I remember how excited I was after completing the first draft. I read the story and revised it at least a dozen times, and I really liked it. I also remember the criticism I received after sharing the story in a writing workshop. Instead of providing guidance on how to improve the story, the instructor suggested that I *change* the story, and quite drastically. I remember she said, "If it were me, I would change the plot altogether and . . ." Well, needless to say, I did not feel very good after that discussion. I thought about the instructor's comments and her possible motivations and I re-read the story many, many times. In the end, I decided I liked the story just the way it was, just the way I wrote it. I could live with that decision, but none other.

I can't say if *No Turning Back* will go down as one of my best or worst stories, or if it will be memorable in any way at all. Only time will tell. Nevertheless, the story will always be a memorable one for me, for it defines me and defines the beginning of my career as a writer. With the story, I deliberately drew a line in the sands of life. I crossed over into a new world where anything is possible. I came upon a crossroads with no signage except for what I was willing to construct and which would provide direction for me and for anyone else who might be interested. I took that first step, and the road before me became clear. I relish the fact that I have no choice but to move forward and take on whatever challenges may come before me, and I know there is no possibility of going in any other direction. There is no turning back.

I dedicate this story to all of the brave men and women who fight for our country, our freedom, and our safety, and I am eternally grateful.

Acknowledgements

I would like to start by thanking the entire Chicago Arts Press family. You were all instrumental in helping me to make this first collection of published short stories a reality. I could not have done it without you, and I am very grateful.

I would like to thank my editors: Kelly O'Connor McNees, Ashley McDonald, and Diane Piron-Gelman, all of whom helped me to perfect my stories.

I would like to thank Vasil Nazar, who did a masterful job formatting the book into its final and publishable form.

I would like to thank Chicago actress and artist Kelly Maryanski, who willingly agreed to read the manuscript and subsequently provided the custom ink illustrations for each of the stories.

I have always believed you can tell a book by its cover, and I was so fortunate to have the opportunity to work with the world-renowned graphic artist, Hugh Syme. Hugh, thank you for your professionalism, guidance, and creativity. What a cover!

Of course, my life revolves around my family, especially my wife and my children. They are the core of what I am and whatever I will become. They realize there is no turning back now, and they are all willing to come along for the ride, wherever the road may take us.

I'm the luckiest guy in the world.

ABOUT THE AUTHOR

Dan Burns is the author of the breakout novel, *Recalled to Life*. In addition to writing novels and short stories, he also writes screenplays for the big screen. His forthcoming novel, *A Fine Line*, is a crime mystery set in his hometown of Chicago.

For more information, please visit www.danburnsauthor.com.

Also by
DAN BURNS

RECALLED TO LIFE

A NOVEL

Chicago architect Peter O'Hara had a plan, a blueprint, for how he wanted to build his life. He had goals and ambitions and his path was clear. He had a loving wife and son, career success, and his final career goal was close within reach. The opportunity to become a partner in his firm was there for the taking. He almost had it all.

But life and fate do not consider such plans. An unbelievable and unplanned event sets off a domino effect of repercussions that turn Peter's life upside down, pushing him to his limits and causing him to re-evaluate everything he thought was important.

"Recalled to Life is a timeless story for all generations."